Also by Susanna Shore

House of Magic
Hexing the Ex
Saved by the Spell
Third Spell's the Charm

P.I. Tracy Hayes
Tracy Hayes, Apprentice P.I.
Tracy Hayes, P.I. and Proud
Tracy Hayes, P.I. to the Rescue
Tracy Hayes, P.I. with the Eye
Tracy Hayes, from P.I. with Love
Tracy Hayes, Tenacious P.I.
Tracy Hayes, Valentine of a P.I.
Tracy Hayes, P.I. on the Scent
Tracy Hayes, Unstoppable P.I.

Two-Natured London
The Wolf's Call
Warrior's Heart
A Wolf of Her Own
Her Warrior for Eternity
A Warrior for a Wolf
Magic under the Witching Moon
Moonlight, Magic and Mistletoes
Crimson Warrior
Magic on the Highland Moor
Wolf Moon
Magic for the Highland Wolf

Thrillers
Personal
The Assassin

Third Spell's the Charm

House of Magic 3

Susanna Shore

Crimson House Books

Third Spell's the Charm
Copyright © 2022 A. K. S. Keinänen
All rights reserved.

The moral right of the author has been asserted.

No part of this book may be reproduced, translated, or distributed without permission, except for brief quotations in critical articles and reviews.

This is a work of fiction. Names, characters, places, dialogues and incidents either are the product of the author's imagination or are used fictitiously. Any resemblance to actual events, organizations or persons, living or dead, except those in public domain, is entirely coincidental.

Book Design: A. K. S. Keinänen
Cover Design: A. K. S. Keinänen
Cover Image: Sergey Myakishev

ISBN 978-952-7061-55-8 (paperback edition)
ISBN 978-952-7061-54-1 (e-book edition)

www.susannashore.com

One

I SET MY HAIR ON FIRE trying to conjure water. Not the intended outcome, but inevitable to my increasing aggravation.

I'd twisted my hands and fingers into correct positions, and recited the required words of the spell, practically tasting the water already. The next thing I knew my hair was burning.

I shrieked and lost concentration, which made the spell break. It didn't quench the fire. That was done by Amber Boyle, who was teaching me spellcasting, with an elegant flick of her long fingers.

Too late. The fire had singed a chunk of my long cinnamon hair that I'd foolishly left down. The stench of burnt hair made me gag and I dreaded to think what my hair looked like.

"That was not supposed to happen," Amber said, baffled by my inadequacy. "A water spell is the opposite of a fire spell."

You don't say…

We were sitting face to face on the polished wooden floor of the workroom in the attic of the House of Magic, a magic shop Amber owned with her wife, Giselle Lynn.

The shop gave name to the entire building in Clerkenwell, Central London, where I was their lodger.

Amber had drawn a protective circle on the floor with chalk and we were inside it. It was supposed to help me focus my magic and prevent accidents.

Apparently it only prevented accidents outside it.

"I told you, this keeps happening," I said miserably.

She tilted her head, making a shock of red curls sway. I bet she'd never accidentally burned her hair with a spell.

She was thirty-eight, tall and reed thin, a former trauma nurse turned full-time magic shop keeper. She was also a mage. And not just any mage. She was the newly minted leader of the Mages' Council that governed all the mages in London.

I was twelve years younger, assistant to an arts and antiques dealer, and a newly minted mage. That was the assumption anyway.

The entire world of magic, mages, and supernatural creatures was new to me. Two months ago, I'd accidentally triggered a curse meant for my boss, Archibald Kane. He was the owner of Kane's Arts and Antiques and also a mage, and he'd had no choice but to reveal their existence to me.

Then I'd learned that my great-aunt Beverly had been a mage too. It wasn't exactly talked openly about with non-mages, and no one in my family knew about it. Since being a mage was hereditary and tended to be matrilinear, Kane had deduced that I must be one as well. I'd been delighted by the prospect of learning to cast spells, and he'd been sure I could learn, even though I was much older than mages usually were when they began.

So far, I'd only managed to prove him wrong.

Third Spell's the Charm

It wasn't for lack of qualified teachers. Amber and Giselle had been happy to help me learn the basics. They were good at it too. Giselle especially had great patience for a complete dunce like me.

For the first three weeks, I'd mostly been reading about the inner workings of spells, how a spell didn't create anything but manipulated existing elements—or molecules, according to modern magic theories—into taking new forms. The books were vague on how it was possible. No one really knew the answer, other than that the ability was something mages were born with. Without it, the spells wouldn't take—ignite or catch, if you will—no matter how much you wiggled your fingers while incanting.

We'd also meditated a lot. Since the ability to manipulate elements was inherent, a mage had to be able to access the place inside them where the potential for it resided. I wasn't entirely sure I'd located mine yet.

This week, we'd finally progressed to the practical aspect of being a mage: spellcasting. I'd imagined myself throwing spells around like Amber, Giselle, and Kane did, merely with some innate mage-ness that would impress everyone.

Amber and Giselle had had other ideas.

"We'll start with conjuring water. It's the easiest spell, as it's one of the basic elements," Amber had told me, then reconsidered: "Or the molecules required for it are the most common and everywhere around us. Whichever theory you like to subscribe to."

"Also the gestures needed for it are the simplest," Giselle had added with her easy smile. "Children start with it too."

Turned out, their notion of easy wasn't compatible with reality. I'd spent two evenings trying to bend and twist my fingers to the exact position needed for the spell. After I'd finally managed it to their satisfaction, I'd had to learn the incantation.

That at least was a simple four-word spell, even if the words weren't any real language but some sort of bastardisation of Latin. According to my teachers, most spells were like that—except the ones based on ancient Greek—which of course only applied to Western magic. Asian magic was mostly based on an old form of Chinese, and there were other traditions too, but I wouldn't be learning those any time soon.

Finally, it was time to put the pieces together to cast the spell. I needed to reach inside for the source of my ability while gesturing with my fingers and saying the words with intent, first aloud and then silently once I'd learned it.

I'd been at it the entire Saturday, alone in the attic. At first, nothing had happened. It had vexed me, but then I'd concentrated anew, dug deep into myself for that special ingredient, and cast the spell with as much purpose as I could muster.

Water should've appeared in the small bowl in front of me. Instead, my hand had burst into flames.

Shrieking, I'd lost my concentration and the fire had died. Luckily there was some sort of failsafe to fire spells that prevented them from damaging the caster's skin. But it had unnerved me, and for the next ten or so tries my spell hadn't caught.

Little by little, I'd begun to relax and concentrate better. That's when the fires started again.

Third Spell's the Charm

First it was my other hand. Then it was a feather on the shelf where Amber and Giselle kept their potion ingredients—the smell was disgusting—and lastly, the notebook for my magic notes. It was in cinders before I even realised it was on fire. Only the tiny magnet that kept the lid closed remained in the pile of ash.

It truly vexed me, and not merely because it was a month's work lost. It had been a really nice hardcover notebook I'd bought from the gift shop in the British Museum, with a picture of *The Great Wave Off Kanagawa* by Hokusai on the cover.

The irony wasn't lost on me.

I'd admitted my defeat, and asked Amber to help. We'd gone through the basics once more, and then she'd asked me to cast the spell again. With the aforementioned result.

"There must be something wrong with your focus, because I can't detect any mistakes in your casting. We'd best meditate. Try to concentrate on the magic inside you."

She tugged the knees of her yoga trousers and settled more comfortably—or as comfortably as one could sitting cross-legged on a polished wooden floor. She closed her eyes and rested her wrists on her knees, palms up.

I mirrored the position. I hadn't meditated before Amber and Giselle had made me, and I wasn't sure I was doing it right. But I tried to calm my mind, and concentrated on my breathing like she'd instructed.

"Do you feel a spark inside you?" she asked when we'd breathed calmly for a couple of minutes.

My stomach growled, and I cringed, opening my eyes. Amber rolled hers, an impressive feat considering she kept them closed.

"Ignore the hunger. Let your mind float until you feel it being pulled somewhere. Then follow it to the source. That's where your magic resides. Study it. It has to become as familiar to you as your breathing."

She'd said the same the first time we did this, and a couple of times since. Problem was, I didn't feel anything pulling my mind. There was nothing inside me.

"You have the spark," Amber said, as if reading my mind. "You couldn't set things on fire if you didn't. You simply need to give it room to emerge. It's a bit shy, so you have to quiet your mind to let it become willing to show itself."

As far as visualisations went, that actually helped. I ignored my hunger—easier said than done when the scents of Giselle's dinner preparations reached the attic—and pushed every emotion and sensation away: the hard floor under my buttocks, my disappointment and frustration, the fear that I wouldn't be a mage after all.

Nothing happened for the longest time. But I waited with more patience than before, maintaining the emptiness of my mind, pushing away the unpleasant sensations like my legs going numb.

And then, between the thin line of awake and not quite asleep, a tug. Or more like a faint flutter that clearly had a direction. Deeper.

Fearing I would lose it, I reached for it and cast the water spell. Too fast. The sensation disappeared, burying itself in the chaos that was my mind once more.

Disappointment made bile rise to my mouth, and I squeezed my eyes tightly so my tears wouldn't show.

Amber cleared her throat, and I opened my eyes.

"Your hair is on fire again, Phoebe."

Third Spell's the Charm

GISELLE HAD TO cut me bangs. My hair was so badly damaged at the front that it was the only solution.

"I look like I'm fifteen," I sighed, staring at my face in the bathroom mirror. My hazel eyes were miserable under the encroaching hairline, and my face looked alien to me. I hadn't had a fringe since I was in school and was required to keep my hair in braids to go with the uniform.

"Better to look fifteen than fifty-five," Giselle said mercilessly, chocolate eyes twinkling and dimples deep with suppressed laughter. She was forty-one, shortish with soft curves, her steel grey hair in a pixie cut I found myself envying. Anything was better than the fringe.

She patted me on the shoulder. "You'll get used to it. Now, let's go eat dinner before it's ruined."

We cleaned the bathroom of the evidence of my incompetence, though I now carried it on my face, and I pulled my hair into a ponytail. It helped a little.

"At least your handiwork is neat," I said to Giselle as we headed down the stairs.

Giselle flashed me her easy smile. "I used to be a hairdresser."

"I didn't know that."

She made a dismissive gesture. "It's not something I remember often. It's been ... almost twenty years since I made a career change to become a cook, before giving that up and becoming a full-time witch after I inherited the shop and this house from my aunt."

Witches, unlike mages, could be ordinary humans too, as it was mostly about potions and herbs. Giselle was both.

"You're an excellent cook too."

The rent included meals, which she prepared. After two months of living here, my clothes had started to feel tight, even though I'd added running to my exercise routine.

Laughing, Giselle crossed the short hallway that doubled as the entrance hall. It opened to a combined kitchen and living room, the two separated by a sturdy oaken dining table that seated ten.

The house was narrow and tall. The shop was on the ground floor, with a basement below and the kitchen and living room right above. Giselle's and Amber's quarters were on the floor above that, and the top floor, before the attic, had two bedrooms and a bath for lodgers, of which I was one. The other was Ashley Grant, a firefighter in her early thirties. She was also a werewolf.

That had taken some getting used to.

The kitchen was cosy and functional, and the living room was filled with Victorian sofas, some of them genuine, floor lamps with tasselled shades, occasional tables, and doilies on every surface. Giselle's aunt had loved crocheting. Two bay windows faced the busy high street below.

The table had already been set for five, which meant the whole household would be present. That didn't often happen. Ashley had twenty-four-hour shifts, after which she usually slept the next day, and Luca only attended the meals served after sunset.

He was a vampire, to my great disbelief. That had taken even more getting used to, especially since I'd never witnessed him do anything vampiric, like show his fangs. His teeth were perfectly ordinary.

However, I had seen him cast impressive spells when we were chased by a hellhound, so I knew he wasn't a mere human. And he avoided the sun at all costs.

Third Spell's the Charm

He resided in the basement, where he had a studio flat with its own bathroom and boarded-over windows to keep the sunlight out. He supported himself with poker and stock trading, both online, and at nights he helped at the shop, which was kept open late for those customers who couldn't face daylight either.

I heard him and Amber climb up the stairs from the shop. It closed for dinners, freeing them both to attend. Luca reached the kitchen first.

He wasn't a tall man, only an inch taller than my five-seven, with a tight, muscled body. He looked like a carefree surfer with a handsome, angular face, sandy blond hair he usually kept in a short ponytail, and laughing green eyes. Only the tan was missing—for obvious reasons. He seemed to be about my age, but if I were to believe him, he was over a hundred years old.

Tonight though, the hair was down and casually tousled. He wore slim-fit, steel-grey trousers with a silvery sheen, and a black mesh T-shirt that revealed all the muscles of his impressive torso.

I'd never seen him exercise, so maybe vampires came with a physique like that. Or maybe he went to a twenty-four-hour gym at nights.

He paused abruptly when he spotted me. "Why aren't you dressed? And what the hell happened to your hair?"

I looked baffled at my black leggings and the soft, long-sleeved T. Since I had no answer for the first question, I answered the latter: "A mishap with a spell. What do you mean, dressed?"

"I sent you several messages," he said, exasperated. "Didn't you read any of them?"

I took a seat at the table. "I've literally been in the attic the whole day. I didn't have my mobile with me."

Amber had confiscated it to ensure my unwavering focus. She pulled it out of her pocket now and handed it to me.

"No one called the whole day."

That was a surprise. My parents usually called on Saturdays, and my girlfriends too, as we were too busy on weekdays for anything other than quick messages.

"What were your messages about?" I asked Luca, opening my phone to check if my friends or parents had left any. The only ones were from Luca. He hadn't exaggerated the number of them. There were at least ten.

"I need you to be my wingman tonight."

Two

I SAT STRAIGHT, STUNNED. "Me?" I tilted my head, taking in his appearance with renewed appreciation. "Explains the clothes though. You don't need a wingman looking like that."

A slow grin spread on his face and he twirled, giving me a good look at the backside too. Very nice.

"It's mating season for vampires," he stated, making Amber sputter and cough out the water she'd just sipped. "It's finally dark enough that I can party to the morning."

"I don't have the energy to party all night," I groaned. He gave me a slow look.

"You're twenty-six. Of course you have the energy."

He wasn't wrong, and I liked to dance too, but that wasn't the issue here. "I've been learning magic the whole day. It's exhausting."

Every spell drained the caster's energy. The bigger the spell, the more it drained, although greater mages could cast more of the bigger ones in a row. Even though my spells hadn't had the desired outcome, I was still spent.

"Can't you take Ashley?"

"Did I hear my name?"

The woman in question strode into the kitchen, immediately dwarfing the rest of us. She was six foot one and all muscle, strong enough to handle her physically demanding job even without the added benefit of being supernaturally strong.

With sharp cheekbones, a straight, commanding nose, and strong black brows over dark eyes, she was a striking sight. Added to that were a bald head she shaved regularly, earrings down both lobes, and piercings in her left eyebrow. If you poured her into leather and latex, she'd make an impressive wingman for Luca.

She halted and pinched her nose with her fingers. "You reek of cologne, Luca. What's going on?"

I hadn't smelled anything. I leaned closer to him, but I had to practically press my nose into his chest, making him roll his eyes, before I detected the sublime scent he wore.

Werewolves truly had more sensitive noses. And vampires too, since the scent was so faint.

"Luca wants to go clubbing and he needs company," I told her.

She shuddered in disgust, like a wolf shaking its fur, an oddly elegant gesture. "I can't go to those places. My ears are too sensitive."

"My ears are sensitive too," Luca protested. "That's what magic's for."

"I can't do magic. If there's music, I'm not going."

Luca gave me a pleading puppy look and managed to melt my resolve even though I knew it was just an act. I sighed.

"Fine, I'll come with you. But I can't pull an overnighter."

He grinned. "That's what you think…"

Third Spell's the Charm

The last time I'd gone clubbing had been months ago. My three best friends and I had celebrated the birthday of one of us in May with an almost overnighter, and we'd had a great time. Back then, I'd believed I was in a happy and secure relationship with Troy Newell, a City banker I'd been seeing for a year. Less than a month after that night, I'd learned that he'd been cheating on me the entire time we were together, and had broken up with him.

Heartbroken, clubbing hadn't exactly been at the top the things I wanted to do, but I'd gone to a club in Nice in August when I visited my parents, who lived near there. It had been a short evening though; I'd mostly wanted to prove to myself that I was over Troy.

I hadn't been.

When I finally recovered from the breakup—it involved a hex I accidentally put on him—and let myself fall for a guy named Jack Palmer, a mage—not that I knew it when I met him—the bastard had put a spell on me that made me repulsive to men. Literally. Being around me had made every man except him nauseated. Even if I had been in a partying mood, I couldn't have gone anywhere near men.

I'd managed to rid myself of the spell, and Jack. The latter possibly also literally, although I did hope he wasn't dead. But I'd been busy with learning to become a mage since, and hadn't even met with my girlfriends, let alone gone clubbing.

It was high time I had a night out. And Luca was always great company.

I was starting to feel excited about the night as I prepared for it after dinner. I selected my outfit carefully. I didn't know if the wingman—or wingwoman—was supposed to look hotter than the chap she was there for, but I didn't want to fade into the background next to Luca either.

The choice was between white trousers that hugged my legs and a powder pink miniskirt of some stretchy material that looked like leather. Trousers would've been weather appropriate—October had been rainy—but since I wanted to pair it with a black, long-sleeved, mesh blouse, I would've been dressed exactly like Luca and that couldn't be.

The skirt it was. I could wear black tights for warmth.

I'd gained a little bit of weight since I'd worn the skirt last, but it still fit and made my bottom look rounder. My cleavage looked better too in the black bra that showed through the shirt.

Maybe I'd keep some of this excess weight after all…

I pulled my hair into a dressier ponytail, the kind with hair wrapped around it, which made the horrid fringe look slightly better. I made my eyes look dark and mysterious—I hoped—and my lips kissable. Not that I had any intentions of kissing anyone.

The footwear was a choice between strappy sandals and knee-high boots of the same leather-like material as the skirt, but black. The sandals would've looked better, but I gave into the weather and wore the boots. They made my legs look good, and since they were almost flat, my feet would thank me later.

As a last-minute addition, I wore a leather jacket too, genuine leather. I left it open—for now.

My efforts were instantly appreciated when I entered the living room, where Luca was waiting. He glanced at me over the backrest of the armchair he was lounging in, then glanced again.

"Wow! You look hot."

Third Spell's the Charm

I twirled around, my cheeks warming. "Thanks. Where do you want to go?"

The club scene in London was varied and vibrant, something for everyone if one knew where to look. My girlfriends and I usually went to the trendiest place, suffered the long queues and ridiculous prices, and declared ourselves satisfied afterwards.

"Let's start with a few cocktail bars and see where that'll lead us."

We took a taxi to Soho, a trendy area in the middle of Central London. It had a lively nightlife and I'd often ended up there with my friends.

We weren't the only people around despite the bleak weather. It was Saturday night in London, and everyone was young at heart. There were queues to every pub and wine bar we wanted to enter. We chose the longest one on the assumption that it had to be the best.

I hoped it didn't merely mean it had the slowest staff.

"So what's the gameplan?" I asked Luca, who tilted his head and considered me with a small smile.

"Would you believe if I said I wanted to get laid?"

I'd sort of assumed that was self-evident. "You don't?"

He shrugged. "Maybe. But mostly I need to feed."

I stepped away from him, the reaction involuntary, and he sneered.

"What, you're frightened by me now?"

A faint blush rose to my cheeks. "No, I was just surprised that you'd talk about it so openly."

He gave me a pointed look. "You know what I am."

"It's just that I didn't believe you." I made a helpless gesture, and his brows shot up.

"Why would I lie about that?"

"Because women are into weird stuff?"

He laughed. "I'll give you that…"

The line moved and we took a few steps forwards. I glanced at Luca from the corner of my eye.

"So … how often do you need to, ummm…?"

He looked amused. "Suck the blood from the veins of an unsuspecting human?"

Gross. "I was about to go with feed, but okay."

"Not often. I can get by with normal food as well. But I need an occasional booster to maintain my … enhancements."

He grinned, reminding me of my ignorance of people other than humans when we first met in August. They'd described themselves as enhanced humans.

"Right. So what am I here for?" I stomped my legs to keep them warm. Despite the tights, the damp air was getting through.

"Your job is to make me look harmless."

I gave him a dubious look. "That doesn't sound predatory at all…"

"Hey, I am a predator." He smiled to soften his words. "But don't worry, my victims will live, and they won't have any memories or visible signs of having been my snack."

That sounded only marginally better.

"And if there's sex, it'll be perfectly consensual, and they'll remember *that* afterwards." His smile was smug now.

"I guess it's not easy being a vampire in this day and age."

"Not as easy as it was in the sixties."

I tilted my head in wry acknowledgement. "I'll have to take your word for that."

Third Spell's the Charm

The queue moved again, bringing us to the open door. We could see that the holdup was a large group of women—not unlike me and my girlfriends—who had ordered complicated cocktails that took forever to make. They looked exotic.

"Want one of those?" I asked Luca, who shrugged.

"Alcohol doesn't really have any effect on me, but you get one."

My mouth dropped. "Why are we bar-hopping, then?"

He grinned. "For fun? To chat up girls? To loosen you up? It's hours until morning. We might as well enjoy the night."

"Can't you just ... mesmerise someone and be done with it?"

He looked appalled. "It's about the chase. I *am* a predator."

"One who hunts the most inebriated at the end of the night?"

"Or the most desperate…"

I laughed. "You and the rest of the blokes."

An arm wrapped around my shoulders just then and a face pressed far too close to mine as a drunken bloke leaned down to speak to me, giving me a whiff of alcohol-soaked breath. Startled, I pulled away, closer to Luca, but the hopeful suitor followed.

"Hello, gorgeous. Why don't you ditch the shorty and we go somewhere just the two of us?"

I made a face, trying to pull away again. "No, thank you."

Luca wrapped an arm around my shoulders, dislodging the eel. A sneer spread on the bloke's face, and he ran his eyes down my body. It would've been more effective if he hadn't lingered on my breasts.

"What, you think you can find someone better?"

"Hope springs eternal."

Luca snorted a laugh, which angered the drunken fool, who leaned closer again. "The lady and I are talking. Bugger off."

"Actually, the lady is very much trying not to talk with you," Luca said. "So you bugger off."

He made a quick gesture with his hand I only noticed because I'd been practicing such gestures lately. The eyes of the harasser glazed over. He shook his head, as if trying to dislodge something in his brain—and walked away.

"That was handy," I said, with an admiring smile. "Can you teach me that too?"

"Sorry, it's a vampire speciality."

Bummer.

The queue finally cleared. I grabbed Luca by his arm and pulled him into the bar with me. "Come, I need a drink."

THREE HOURS AND FAR too many bars—and drinks—later, we were queueing to a nightclub. The cold had stopped bothering me three drinks ago, and I was having a brilliant time. I was dancing in the queue with the people around me, each to music only they could hear.

Mine was Abba, by the way. Really danceable, and I vaguely heard it playing in the club every time the door opened. I had no idea where we were, but since we hadn't walked all that much, I was pretty sure we were still in Soho or thereabouts.

"What is this place?" I asked Luca, looking around. I was slurring a little and had trouble focusing my eyes. I

Third Spell's the Charm

narrowed them to see better and spotted a rainbow flag over the door.

"Is this ... a gay club?"

He grinned. He'd been wonderful company the whole night, and seemed to be having a good time too, even though I'd probably been a lousy wingman. "It is."

"And are you...?"

I'd been pretty sure he preferred women. He certainly showed great appreciation to my body, and he'd only chatted up women all night.

His grin deepened. "Anything goes. For sex and for food. Except vampires." He shuddered, disgusted. I decided not to probe that particular ghost. "And I'm sure you'll be more comfortable here too."

The drunken fool at the first bar hadn't been the only drunken fool that evening, keeping Luca's mesmerising skills busy.

I wrapped an arm around his. "Aww, thanks."

The queue was mercifully short, as I was starting to feel cold again. I was underdressed for a gay club too. If I'd known we'd come here, I'd have worn more glittery clothes and larger jewellery. And a feather boa.

I envied the plush pink thing the person in front of me had wrapped around their throat. I bet it warmed nicely. I tapped on their shoulder.

"I'll give you five pounds for that boa," I said, trying to sound sharp.

They turned around and revealed themself to be a tall and fabulous drag queen in a sequined dress and gravity defying heels. She lifted a well-painted brow and tilted her head, checking me out with her cherry lips pursed.

"It would bring your outfit together perfectly."

"I know!"

She took off the boa and wrapped it around my throat with great artistry. Then she offered me the crook of her arm and I took it.

"What's your name, hon?"

"Phoebe, and this is Luca."

"I'm Miss Peaches."

She offered her free hand to Luca, who dutifully—and elegantly—bowed over it, placing a small kiss on it.

"Charmed," he drawled.

"Oooh, you have an old school gentleman here."

I nodded, proud of him like he was my creation. "Considering he's over a hundred years old, he's definitely old school."

Both of her brows shot up. "He's well preserved for such an old chap."

"That's because he's a vampire," I stage whispered. Luca shook his head, exasperated, and Miss Peaches gave a throaty laugh.

"I've always wanted to meet one."

"Tonight's your lucky night, then."

"You don't say…"

She offered her other arm to Luca, who took it. "So what does a vampire do for a living?"

"Stock trading."

"That is *so* boring," she said, her shoulders slumping.

Luca's mouth quirked. "What do you do, then?"

"I'm an entertainer." She pulled out a calling card from her bra and handed it to him. "I can be hired for all kinds of occasions, and I perform regularly at a cabaret in *Brasserie Noël*.

"I've always wanted to see one of those!" I often had lunch there, as it was near where I worked—and near

Third Spell's the Charm

where we currently were too, come to think of it—but I'd never had a chance to see any of the shows.

Then again, I'd been avoiding the place lately, because Jack had taken me there on our one and only date.

Miss Peaches jumped excitedly. "You absolutely have to come on Tuesday! I'll put your names on the list. There are shows tomorrow too, but I'm not performing, so don't come then."

Happy with the prospect, we queued five more minutes until we reached the door. A large bouncer guarded it, built like the Rock and with a similar bald head too. But instead of reminding me of the actor, he reminded me of...

"Are you related to Ashley?" I asked him with the frankness of an inebriate, leaning closer. He had the same sharp cheekbones and regal nose, though his was much larger. His black brows shot up and I could easily imagine them with piercings.

"Who's asking?" he said, and even his voice reminded me of her, though it was much deeper and rougher. His nostrils flared, like Ashley's when she was smelling something unpleasant, and he curled his upper lip at Luca. I guess werewolves didn't like vampires except in our house.

"I'm Phoebe Thorpe, and this is Luca. We're her housemates," I gushed, excited for guessing right. "Miss Peaches here doesn't live in our house. We only just met her."

He studied me, bemused. "Ashley's my sister."

"I knew it!" I jumped up and down. "What's your name?"

"I'm ... Ronnie."

"Is it short for Ronald?"

"No, just Ronnie." He pulled the door open, practically throwing us in. "Have a nice night."

Three

THE DOOR BANGED CLOSED behind us, leaving us in near darkness until my eyes adjusted. We were in a tiny foyer with a cloakroom on one side and cashier's desk by the stairs down. Luca paid us all in, much to the delight of Miss Peaches.

The club itself was below ground, down a flight of steep stairs. It was hot and loud, and I was beginning to regret the feather boa, so I gave it back to Miss Peaches, wrapping it around her neck. She needed to bend quite low for me to manage it. Not because she was that much taller, but because I was slightly uncoordinated.

"Let's dance," she said, dragging me to the dance floor.

It was good-sized, but full of people. It didn't stop us. She cut through the floor with sheer determination, and I found myself in the middle of it, pressed from all sides by bodies swaying and hopping to the beat.

I lost Luca, but I figured a man his age knew how to take care of himself without me. I was having a great time. Music was great, the company was great, and the people dancing around me were great. No one tried to grope me once.

I soon lost Miss Peaches in the throng of the dance floor too, but that didn't stop me from enjoying myself. I danced to exhaustion, leaving the heartache and stress of the past couple of months behind. I was refreshed and rejuvenated.

And thirsty.

Pushing through the wall of dancers, I made my way to the bar and bought myself a large glass of water. I'd had enough alcohol for one night.

I leaned my back against the bar, ignoring the people who were trying to push me aside, and searched the crowd for Luca or Miss Peaches, but couldn't find either. Not a big surprise. It was a large place, and the lighting was a combination of near dark and coloured spots, so you couldn't really see anyone farther than your arm's length.

The person *at* arm's length from me was an attractive man about a decade older than me, in sleek trousers and a formfitting white shirt with the collar unbuttoned. I considered making a move, but the odds that he would be the only straight man here weren't great.

He was tall and leanly built, with a narrow, classically defined face and Roman nose. His wavy hair was combed back and reached to the collar of his jacket, and it was such dark auburn that it appeared black in the dim light.

He was studying the crowd too, but not like he was looking for a good time. More like checking the wares and not finding anything worth his while. He noticed me staring at him—I was too drunk to be subtle about it—and turned his attention to me.

A powerful stare hit me with such force that I staggered back. I'd only once experienced a similar demonstration of magical strength, with a warlock called

Third Spell's the Charm

Laurent Dufort; a frightening man who practiced forbidden black magic.

If this man was a warlock too, I'd best beat a hasty retreat.

I finished my water with one gulp, put the empty glass on the bar, and headed towards the loo like I'd meant to do that all along and wasn't fleeing. Although once I reached the end of the queue outside the toilets, I realised I did need to go.

Twenty minutes later—toilet queues in these places always took forever—I returned relieved and convinced that I'd imagined the impact the man had on me. I glanced at the bar, but he wasn't there anymore.

It was time to find Luca. I'd neglected him for hours and I was supposed to be his wingwoman.

It was impossible to find anyone on the dance floor, so I began to circle the sides of the room where there were tables and booths, all occupied. They were shrouded in darkness, and I tried to peer through it to see if one of them held Luca, but I only managed to witness some blush-inducing scenes. I moved hastily on, pretending I hadn't seen anything.

Finally, in the back corner, I spotted Miss Peaches. She was alone in a booth and appeared to be sleeping, slumped against the corner, her head lolling forward. Or she'd passed out, though she hadn't seemed drunk the last I saw her.

I slid onto the seat next to her and reached for her shoulder. "Wake up, sweetie. It's time to get you home."

Her head tilted to the side, revealing a long neck under the feather boa. There was something dark on it, and I leaned in to take a closer look.

Blood!

Startled, I pulled back. With a shaking hand I reached for her wrist to feel the pulse there, but couldn't find it. Sick with worry, I pulled down the boa to study her neck again—and my heart made a sickening lurch.

There were two puncture marks on the large vein. I'd never seen similar in real life, but I'd seen enough of them on screen.

Bite marks.

Miss Peaches had been killed by a vampire. And there was only one in the house…

I scrambled hastily out of the booth. I needed help, but I didn't know who to turn to. Someone at the bar, maybe?

A hand grabbed my wrist and started to pull me forwards. I was so stunned I didn't even resist at first. And then I saw who it was. Luca.

"Where are you going? We need to find help. Miss Peaches is dead."

He glanced back, his face grim. "I know."

I paused, forcing him to pause too, though in truth he could've easily forced me to continue. I leaned almost to his face so that I wouldn't have to shout over the music.

"She was killed by a vampire."

"I know."

I pulled back, stunned. "You admit it?"

"It wasn't me," he practically growled.

"What?"

He began to pull me away again, and I complied. He didn't pause but dragged me all the way out of the club. The cold night air hit me with force, clearing my head, and I stopped again.

"We can't flee."

This time he pulled me on. "We have to."

Third Spell's the Charm

"Why?"

"Because I'm not the only vampire here."

"WHAT DOES THAT MEAN?" I demanded. He glanced around, his eyes large and spooked.

"Not here."

Giving in, I followed him to the closest high street, where we could get a taxi. It was another long queue, but that was London nightlife for you.

Luca kept glancing around as we queued, tense, as if fearing someone would attack him at any moment. I was jumpy too, expecting the police to come arrest us.

I couldn't believe we'd just left Miss Peaches there. My stomach was roiling for what I'd witnessed and my actions. Even if Luca had to flee other vampires, surely I could've stayed.

I was fighting tears by the time we got into a cab.

At home, he led me to his room in the basement. I was exhausted, the joyous bounce that had kept me partying gone, but I wanted to hear what he had to say.

His room was the usual mess of discarded clothes, dirty teacups, empty soda cans, and unmade bed, but I couldn't muster the energy to care. I sat on his bed and waited for him to speak.

Luca began to pace the room, running a hand down his face a few times. He was pale and sweating. I didn't even know vampires could sweat—or get any paler.

Then again, I didn't know anything about vampires.

Finally, he paused and faced me. "I haven't been entirely honest with you."

Fear arrested my breath. *Please, don't let him confess to killing Miss Peaches after all...*

"I've sort of ... implied that I'm the only vampire around here. And I let you understand that when vampires feed, we only take a few sips and the victim can go on living, none the wiser."

He paused, and I waited for him to get to the point. He averted his gaze briefly, before mustering the strength to look me in the eyes.

"Neither is true. There are hundreds of us in London alone, and we are the monsters of the stories who drain their victims until they die."

I must've paled, or he detected a skip in my heartbeat, because he lifted a calming hand.

"Except me. Now."

He began to pace again, kicking the discarded clothes from his path as he went.

"Back when I was turned into a vampire, I was like the rest. Interested only in the hunt, preying on the helpless and killing them." His lip curled in disgust. "I have no excuse, though it's inherent in being a vampire. But it stopped feeling like me at some point, a decade later, maybe. I began to feed more seldom, but even then I drained my victims to death. When my skills with magic became greater, I learned to manipulate human minds and heal the puncture wounds. After that, I haven't needed to kill my victims."

I nodded, understanding, and he continued.

"Stupidly, I began to tell other vampires about it. How we didn't have to be monsters anymore. But it turned out they liked being monsters. So I was ... ostracised."

I had a feeling there was more to it than not being invited to Christmas parties anymore, but I didn't probe.

"I'm ... sorry."

Third Spell's the Charm

He shrugged. "I'm better without them, even if it's been a bit lonely sometimes not being able to share what I am. I was lucky when I met Amber and Giselle, who believed I was a different beast. It helps that I don't have to hide my true self here."

My heart ached for him. "So what does that have to do with tonight?"

"By an unspoken decree, other vampires and I avoid each other. It's easy, since I seldom hunt. And if the worst happens and we end up at the same place, we both usually leave."

I nodded. "Except tonight?"

He spread his arms. "There were so many people in that club that I couldn't sense other vampires. I would've taken you away if I had."

I nodded again and he continued.

"Whether we give each other room or not, we don't feed in public. And we don't leave our victims in public places with clear signs of our actions. We can't risk the exposure it would bring."

"So why did they? Were they interrupted?"

"I don't know."

"So why did you have to leave?"

He gestured helplessly with his hands. "A vampire who doesn't care about our rules is bad news. If it's someone who hates me, they might harm me—or you."

My heart skipped another beat in fear. "Do you think they know you were there?"

He shook his head. "I don't know. But I couldn't sense them, so they probably couldn't sense me."

"How long until they find the body? And what then?"

He slumped on the bed next to me. "If we're lucky, not until after closing time, when there won't be so many people around. They'll likely call the police, and then the detectives will have a bizarre case on their hands. The tabloids will have a field day."

I could already see the headlines screaming of vampire attacks.

"The bouncer knows you're a vampire. He'll send the police after you."

"What could he say? That he knows the vampire who did it? Werewolves need secrecy as much as we do. He won't send anyone after us."

That was only a small consolation. Miss Peaches was dead and there was a killer vampire at large.

I rubbed my face, trying to stay awake. It jolted a memory loose. My heart stopped. "I think I met the vampire tonight."

He stilled. "What? Are you sure?"

"I thought he was a warlock. He was certainly powerful and … dark. But he could've been a vampire too."

Luca ran a hand over his mouth. "Fuck. You could've ended up as his victim."

"Yeah…"

"What did he look like?"

That was easy. His image was seared in my mind. "Tall, handsome, hawkish nose and lush, amber hair."

He crossed his fingers behind his neck, bending down until his head hit his knees. "Shiiit… That's Morgan Hunt."

"Who's he?"

"He's the most powerful vampire in London and our de facto leader. Such as we have. He's bad news."

My head was spinning. I lay down on the bed, trying not to throw up. I closed my eyes to keep the room still.

Third Spell's the Charm

Little by little, my gut eased, and my breathing slowed down.

I JOLTED AWAKE, startling Griselda, the grey cat who reigned supreme in our house. She'd been wrapped around my head, sleeping. She shot me an offended glare from her emerald eyes and jumped down, heading out of the room.

I realised only then that I wasn't in my own room. I was in Luca's bed, fully clothed but without the boots. He'd removed them and lifted my legs onto the bed, so that I hadn't slept with them hanging over the edge like when I'd fallen asleep.

I'd been figuratively dead to the world and had probably slept in the position he had left me, not stirring once. My body was stiff.

Luca was under the duvet on the other side of the bed, chest bare—and presumably without other clothes too—sleeping. I resisted the urge to check if he was breathing or if vampires were truly dead during the day.

It *was* day already, even though the blocked windows didn't let any light in; the clock on the wall told me it was almost eleven in the morning. Carefully, so as not to disturb Luca—though I don't know why I bothered—I rose from the bed, picked up my boots, and headed upstairs.

The shop was closed on Sundays, and it was dark. I climbed to the next floor, and sounds and scents of cooking reached me. I paused to check whether I was too hungover to eat. My head was aching a little, but I wasn't feeling sick. Leaving the boots on a shoe rack in the hallway, I decided to give it a try.

Three curious faces met me when I entered the kitchen and slow smiles spread on all when they took in my appearance. "Are you coming home only now?" Amber asked, tilting her head.

"You reek of the vampire," Ashley stated. "Did you sleep with him?"

I sat at the table, groaning. "No, and not the way you think. I fell asleep in his room."

"The question then becomes why were you in his room in the first place?" Giselle teased me, placing a cup of tea in front of me. She had teas for all occasions, for which she grew the herbs herself. This one smelled like it could cure nausea, peppermint the most prominent scent.

I took a heaven-sent gulp, debating what to tell them. But they were my friends and the only people with whom I could talk about this. Besides, Amber would want to know if vampires started leaving bodies out in the open.

Tears sprang to my eyes out of the blue, startling everyone, including me. "A vampire killed a woman in the club last night."

Everyone startled, then turned stunned and angry. "Luca would never kill anyone," Amber stated with an affirmative slash of her hand.

"It wasn't him."

"Who, then?" Ashley demanded.

"And why?" Giselle added. She placed a plate of scrambled eggs in front of me, and even though I didn't feel like eating, I picked up a fork and began to shovel it into my mouth.

"Luca has no idea why," I said between mouthfuls. "But he thinks it's someone called Morgan Hunt."

"I've heard of him," Amber said, looking grim. "He's the most powerful vampire in the country. And not just in magic and strength, but in wealth and influence among humans too."

I shook my head, baffled. "Why would he publicly kill someone, then?"

That stymied us.

"What club was it?" Ashley asked.

"This gay club in Soho."

"Was my brother a bouncer there?"

I perked. I'd forgotten the whole thing. "He was! He looks just like you. I recognised him instantly." A lump of ice dropped into my stomach. "Could you ask him what's been done with the body?"

Ashley got up. "I'll give him a ring."

In defiance of millennials everywhere, she never carried her mobile with her, so she headed upstairs to make the call. I finished eating and was on my second cup of tea before she returned. She looked baffled.

"Ronnie said there was no body. He should know. He's the one who checks the house after the doors are closed."

Four

MY MOUTH DROPPED OPEN. "I know what I saw."

Or did I?

"Luca saw it too."

Ashley looked grim. "Ronnie said he hadn't detected other vampires in the house either."

"Then what happened to Miss Peaches? She had no pulse and there were bite marks and blood on her throat."

Ashley spread her arms, out of suggestions. Amber tapped her upper lip.

"A prank? It's almost Halloween."

My heart skipped a beat. A part of me wanted to hope Miss Peaches was alive and laughing at Luca and me somewhere. But I shook my head.

"I couldn't find a pulse. And how could she have pulled off a prank like that in such short notice?"

I had a vague, embarrassing recollection of telling her Luca was a vampire, so maybe she had.

"Then someone else killed her, made it look like a vampire did it, and then hid the body," Giselle suggested. "The question remains who and why though."

"Could it have been a warlock? I did meet that powerful man, and if there weren't other vampires around, he wasn't Morgan Hunt."

Amber looked grim. "I hope not. There aren't any in town that we know of, but I'll talk with Archibald."

My boss, Archibald Kane, was the former leader of the Mages' Council. He was currently studying to become an archmage. They were the most powerful mages, and for that reason weren't allowed to lead the council. Something about absolute power corrupting absolutely, I think.

"Maybe there was another vampire and he mesmerised Ronnie so that he doesn't remember them," Giselle suggested. But Ashley shook her head, vehemently.

"Vampires aren't able to mess our minds with magic."

"He could've been on a break when the other vampire arrived," I suggested. Tears sprang to my eyes again.

"I only met Miss Peaches in the queue to the club, but she was a wonderful person and I want to know what happened to her."

Giselle patted me on the shoulder. "Why don't you go take a shower and maybe a nap. Everything will look better after that."

Since Miss Peaches was (most likely) dead, I didn't think I'd be able to sleep. But I desperately needed both, so I headed upstairs.

When I woke up, it was to an overcast, rainy afternoon. I ambled to the kitchen, and to my surprise found Luca there.

"You're up early."

Third Spell's the Charm

He gave me a tired smile. "Perks of autumn. Shorter and darker days. I can even venture outside too, if I wear a hat."

"And an umbrella," I added dryly, making him laugh.

I sat next to him and pulled him into a one-armed hug. He rested his head on my shoulder for a moment, before sitting up. He gave me a searching look.

"How are you holding up?"

I wanted to cry again, but now wasn't the time. "I just wish we didn't have to leave her like that. Did you talk with others?"

"Yeah, but I don't believe it was a prank. I couldn't detect a pulse. She didn't leave the club on her own."

Hearing that I hadn't imagined it made matters only marginally better. Because it meant Miss Peaches was truly dead and the body had disappeared.

"What should we do?"

He pulled out a calling card from his pocket. It was pink with silver letters. "This is the card Miss Peaches gave me. I think we should go meet her manager and ask if they know her family. We need to let them know what's happened to her."

The prospect made me queasy. "We can't tell them she was killed by a vampire, can we?"

"No. And since there's no body, we can't really say she's dead either. I'll think of something."

"Can we do it tonight?" I didn't want to postpone the upsetting task.

He glanced at his watch. "I think we should go immediately. There's a matinee at Brasserie Noël today, and according to this card the manager can be found there."

"If you truly can go out at this time of day?" He nodded and I pushed up. "Let's go, then. I want to get this over with."

BRASSERIE NOËL WAS LOCATED by a small plaza a short stretch north from Piccadilly Circus where the closest Tube station was. The restaurant on the street level offered quality French food remarkably cheap, and the cabaret was below ground.

The restaurant was full, but the maître d at the door smiled at us and told she could find us a table if we would wait fifteen minutes.

Luca nodded. "Thank you, but we're looking for Maxim Shepard. Is he here today?"

If the woman was disappointed that we weren't here to eat, she didn't show it. "He should be. Go downstairs and enquire there."

The matinee had just ended, and the place had mostly emptied. Some people were still lingering at the cloak room, collecting their raincoats and umbrellas. They would need them. Ours were dripping water on the faded carpet even though we'd tried to shake them dry.

An usher in a wine-red velvet uniform with gold trimmings was closing the wide double doors to the theatre. We approached him, and Luca asked after Maxim Shepard again.

The man spoke to a microphone on the label of his coat, then nodded to us. "He'll see you right away."

He led us to a door at the back of the lobby and opened it with a key card. Behind it was a long hallway with doors on one side and steep concrete steps up at the end. The hallway was empty, but cheerful sounds from

Third Spell's the Charm

behind the doors indicated that the performers were in their dressing rooms winding down after the show.

"Go two floors up. His office is the first on the right at the top."

We did as instructed, my gut tightening as I followed Luca up the stairs. The door to Maxim Shepard's office was open, but Luca gave the frame a knock anyway as we entered.

The small room was filled to overflowing with files and folders, scripts and scores, all stacked in haphazard piles on every available surface and topped with nylon wigs, sequined costumes, and posters of past shows. It smelled of cheap perfume and ancient cigarette smoke that had permeated the walls and curtains.

There was barely room for a desk by the window. A man in his late thirties was sitting behind the desk, legs lifted on the desk, talking on the phone, but he gestured for us to walk deeper, which we did, winding gingerly around the precarious piles. The guest chairs were under the piles too, so we remained standing.

Mr Shepard was dressed in black jeans with a black T-shirt under a red leather blazer, revealing a sturdy but tight body, much like those of gymnasts. He was ordinary looking, with a clean-shaven face and dust brown hair that was thinning a little: unmemorable but not unpleasant to look at.

He ended his call, sat up and smiled at us, giving us a once over. We probably weren't the kind of people he'd been expecting, because his brows furrowed.

"Sorry to keep you waiting. I'm Maxim Shepard. How may I help you?"

Luca and I glanced at each other, and I nudged him with my elbow. Being an assistant to an antiques dealer had not prepared me for delivering bad news. Vampires dealt with death all the time.

He cleared his throat. "We're here on ... behalf of Miss Peaches, whom I believe works for you?"

"Yes." Mr Shepard's gaze sharpened. "You're not here to poach her, are you?"

"No, I ... we..." Luca was clearly struggling to find the right words. He heaved a sigh. "I'm afraid to tell you that Miss Peaches has died."

I stiffened, but it was too late now. Mr Shepard blinked.

"I see." His eyes skimmed over his cluttered desk, as if searching for something. "When? Are you his—her—family?"

"Last night, and no. We didn't know her, but happened to be there when..." Luca paused. "Anyway, we're trying to locate her next of kin. She didn't have a phone or ID with her, only your card."

We had no idea if that was true—who left home without either?—but it was a good excuse.

"Would you like me to inform them?"

Luca hesitated. "Thank you. But I think we'd best do it ourselves, since we were there."

Mr Shepard nodded, and turned to his laptop that barely fit on the corner of his overflowing desk, and clicked it a few times. He frowned.

"It appears there's no address or next of kin in our system."

I startled. "How so?"

He shook his head. "I don't know the details, but if I recall, there was a breakup of a romantic relationship a couple of weeks ago and Miss Peaches moved out and removed the guy as the contact information. She's been

Third Spell's the Charm

staying with friends until she can find a new place." He stilled. "I guess that's not necessary anymore..."

We gave him a moment to recover.

"Her legal name is Sam Selby, when out of drag, in case the police can find the family for you. But I'll ask around with the performers here if they know where she lived, or if anyone knows about the family. If I could get your contact information...?"

Luca gave his email address. "Would it be possible not to share the news with your performers just yet? In case one of them reaches out to the family before we've had a chance to break the news to them?"

"Absolutely. There's a show tonight, and I wouldn't ruin it with such sad news."

That was one way to see it.

We thanked the man and headed out. There was another flight of stairs a little way down the hall from Mr Shepard's office, and we took them down to the restaurant. It was slightly less full now, and I looked around as we crossed the floor to the door. A man caught my attention at a table near the window, his profile clear and recognisable. I grabbed Luca's arm.

"That's the man from the club yesterday."

He stiffened. "Definitely Morgan Hunt. Who's he with?"

We hurried past the maître d, keeping an eye on Hunt's table until we were able to see the face of his companion. My heart stopped.

Archibald Kane. My boss.

MY BOSS'S EYES MET mine across the restaurant floor and they crinkled at the corners as he smiled at me, only to grow large and bewildered when Luca pushed me out of the door. I barely had time for an apologetic wave and then we were already rushing through the rain, belatedly opening our umbrellas.

I'd never fled from my boss before and I wasn't entirely sure why I was doing so now, other than for Luca's fear of Morgan Hunt.

"Slow down," I said exasperated, as Luca pulled me away from the restaurant and in the wrong direction from the Tube station. "Hunt didn't turn to look."

"He doesn't have to lay eyes on me to know I was there. Vampires can sense each other."

"You didn't sense him yesterday."

"I didn't sense him today either," he said, his face grim. "Some vampires are so powerful they can mask their presence from other vampires. I've never met one before though. That I know of," he added gloomily.

I couldn't quite understand why it worried him so much. "Are vampires generally a threat to one another?"

"We're predators and we're territorial, so it's always wise to know where others of my kind are, and doubly so with someone like Hunt for someone like me."

I could definitely understand that.

"How come he's so powerful?" I had to practically run to keep up with him, skipping puddles that had formed on the pavement.

"Age. A vampire doesn't get as powerful as he is overnight."

"He's older than you?"

"Definitely."

"And you're … a little over a hundred?" I guessed, based on his stories as a law pupil in the twenties. The *nineteen* twenties.

Third Spell's the Charm

He finally slowed down, and a small smile tugged the corner of his mouth. "Close enough. But I don't look a day older than twenty-five."

We grinned and I sensed him to relax.

"What was Kane doing with him?" I then had to ask.

The two had looked relaxed and comfortable in each other's company, like they were good friends. I didn't know much about Kane outside of work, and none of his friends, but why would he be friends with a vampire?

Luca shrugged. "They're leaders of the supernatural community. And they're both businessmen. Maybe they have business dealings with each other. Or they belong to the same gentlemen's club or something."

"What, Hunt's been a member of White's since forever?" I found the notion kind of romantic, but he shook his head.

"We change identities regularly. It would be impossible to continue the membership afterwards."

I shot him a curious look. "Have you changed your identity?"

"Naturally. I've only been Luca Marlow for about … ten years."

"Who were you before?"

He gave me an admonishing look. "I'm not telling you. That person is legally dead. Poor thing perished in a car accident."

"Aww. Did he leave a lot of mourners?"

He shook his head. "Not a single one."

I wrapped an arm around his. "Well, the next time you need to change identities, Luca will definitely be mourned."

"Thanks."

He turned a corner and I looked around, baffled. "The closest Tube station is the other way."

"The club is on the next street over. We should take a look at the place ourselves."

"Is it open on Sundays?"

Turned out it was, though the door had only opened fifteen minutes earlier and the place was empty. There was no one at the door or the ticket desk, so we went straight downstairs. Lights were low, but the music wasn't on yet. The place looked strange and much smaller than the previous night when it had been filled with people.

Ronnie was at the bar, leaning against it as he chatted with the young woman organising the glasses behind it. He straightened when he spotted us, and crossed the floor to us. He looked stern, but not like he would attack us for the murder; more a default expression.

"What brings you here?"

"We want to see where Miss Peaches died to figure out how the body was moved." I couldn't think of her as Sam Selby, even if Miss Peaches was only a stage name.

"I think I know how," Ronnie said. "Follow me."

He headed to the booth at the back as if he knew exactly where Miss Peaches had died. It probably smelled of blood or something that only a werewolf could detect. Though how he could scent anything over the stench of stale beer, cheap perfumes, and other smells that permanently stuck to the place was beyond me.

"There's a fire exit right behind this booth," Ronnie explained, rounding the high backrest that I'd taken for a wall, as it reached all the way to the ceiling.

There was a short corridor behind it, wide and deep enough for two people side by side. It was completely

Third Spell's the Charm

dark, save for a green exit light above a blast door at the back.

"I didn't notice this yesterday," I told Luca, who tilted his head in acknowledgement.

"It's usually full of people necking, and difficult to notice," Ronnie explained. "But without a key, it only opens with the emergency latch, and that causes an alarm."

There was a plastic cover over the latch and it was intact.

He swiped a key card to a reader by the door and pushed it open from a large horizontal handlebar designed to make the door open easily in emergency. There was a short hallway on the other side, with steps up at the other end. We climbed up and went through a door at the top to the back alley, next to large bins and a couple of cars.

I looked around. "The vampire could've easily taken Miss Peaches out through here and into a waiting car."

"Except he would've triggered the alarm," Ronnie said.

Luca shook his head. "Not if he was Hunt. He's powerful enough to disable it."

"Morgan Hunt?" Ronnie asked, stunned. "Why would he kill anyone in his own club?"

Our mouths dropped open. "Hunt owns this club?" I asked.

He looked puzzled by our reaction. "Yeah. He owns several clubs, though on the downlow. They're not exactly his main business."

"That would explain why he was here last night," Luca said. "Why did you tell Ashley there weren't other vampires present?"

Ronnie shrugged. "Didn't know he was here. He uses the staff door." He pointed at the door next to the one we'd exited. "But he was the only one."

"That you could detect," I pointed out. "Maybe a different vampire came in through this door."

Ronnie furrowed his brows. "I don't like that idea, but if vampires can handle alarms, I guess it's possible."

"But I didn't detect any vampires either," Luca said.

I gave him a pointed look. "You just told me that if a vampire is strong enough, they can mask their presence from other vampires."

His mouth pressed into a tight line. "But there aren't many of them. One vampire that powerful is bad enough. Two of them..." He let the sentence hang, but I got the idea.

"Mr Hunt didn't kill that person," Ronnie stated with confidence.

"And Luca didn't either," I added with the same conviction.

Luca shook his head. "So there was a third vampire in the club? One we knew nothing about."

"That's quite a theory," a male voice drawled behind us. "Can you prove it too?"

Five

STARTLED, WE PIVOTED TO FACE the newcomer—expect Ronnie, who was facing the right way already.

Morgan Hunt. And he wasn't alone. Kane was with him, looking at me with a slightly raised brow, as if asking why I had fled earlier.

I had no explanation, so I settled for an apologetic grimace.

Archibald Kane, or Kane as he insisted I call him—and who could blame him—was thirty-five, tall, and surprisingly fit under his precise clothing: blue jeans, a crisp white shirt with its collar open, and a brown corduroy jacket tonight—quite a change in style from his usual three-piece suits.

His black hair was thick and combed back, and it tended to billow like it was powered by its own wind, which I'd recently realised happened when he cast spells. His handsome face was lean and defined, and his eyes were deep blue.

He looked and behaved like an old school gentleman most of the time, but I'd witnessed him perform impressive magical feats that had changed my view of him. Underneath his precise behaviour he was a power to reckon with. With him here, Hunt didn't scare me quite as much.

He didn't have a similar effect on Luca, who tensed, eyeing Hunt warily. "Why would I have to prove anything?"

"A vampire killed a person in my nightclub, and you were the only vampire there," Hunt drawled, his cold eyes trained on Luca.

He looked even more impressive in daylight, his suit slim-fit and fashionable, and his auburn hair neatly combed back to give me a good view of his handsome face. His voice was a pleasant tenor that compelled one to pay attention to it.

Then the same dark power I'd sensed the previous night hit me, and I had to brace myself not to step behind Luca. I lifted my chin in defiance that was all bravado.

"Luca is not the vampire you're looking for."

He tilted his head and ran his gaze down my body. "You're the little mage from last night. Do you know what your friend did?"

"He did not kill Miss Peaches!"

His face hardened. "How would you know? You were in the loo when she was killed."

That he'd paid attention to my whereabouts stunned me, and I struggled to come up with a suitable answer. "How would you know when she was killed if you didn't do it yourself?"

Hunt's power flared again and this time I stepped back. Kane cleared his throat. "I don't think this conversation is constructive. Why don't we go somewhere more comfortable and start again?"

Third Spell's the Charm

I didn't want to go anywhere with Hunt. The power he emanated was unnerving, and his accusations were infuriating, but I wanted to find out what had happened to Miss Peaches, and this was Hunt's club.

Hunt gestured at Ronnie, who opened the staff door. There was a short hallway behind it, with offices and staff dressing rooms. Apparently it was my night of visiting backstages of entertainment establishments.

At the other end, a door led back into the club, but this time above the dance floor. It was a small VIP area I hadn't even noticed the previous night. It had low, lush seats, a good view over the club, its own bar, and a loo at the back. It was dark, but Ronnie switched on a light above the bar and we took seats near it.

Hunt sat on a wide sofa, leaning back with arms stretched on the backrest and long legs crossed at the ankles, to all appearances perfectly relaxed and here only to humour us. Luca and I chose a smaller sofa on the other side of a low table, sitting tightly side by side as if seeking safety. Kane sat on a settee next to us, looking calm and in charge, even though this was Hunt's show.

Ronnie brought over a bottle of Scotch and four glasses, and poured a measure in each, leaving the bottle on the low table before retreating behind the bar again. I resisted the urge to snatch the glass and empty it in one go. I needed to calm my nerves, but I needed to keep my wits even more.

Hunt regarded us with a raised brow. "I know of course Mr ... Marlow is it these days?" Luca nodded and he continued: "But I haven't had the pleasure of this young lady."

"And you won't," I stated, making a slow sneer spread on his face.

"Never say never…"

Kane took a sip of his scotch. "Miss Thorpe is my assistant."

Hunt glanced at him. "In magic?"

"At my shop."

Hunt's attention returned to me. "Pleasure, I'm sure."

"And all yours."

A small smile quirked his lips, but there was no true amusement in it. "It appears I've made a poor impression on you."

I glared at him. "You could say that, accusing my friend of a murder."

Hunt's face turned cold, and a shiver of fear ran down my spine. "A person was killed by a vampire in my club. He's a vampire and he was here."

"I didn't kill her," Luca protested, finally finding his voice. Hunt shifted his attention to him.

"Neither did I."

"And when it's word against word, yours is what we'll believe?" I didn't bother to control my anger even though Kane placed a calming hand on my arm. Anger was better than fear.

Hunt's power flared again, pressing against me, making it difficult to breathe. Kane made a quick series of gestures and the pressure eased.

"I would prefer you didn't try that again," he said calmly, but his blue eyes were hard and his hair was billowing with the magic he was wielding to shield us from Hunt's efforts to intimidate us.

Hunt shrugged one shoulder. A moment later Kane's hair settled to its normal position, indicating that Hunt had powered down and Kane didn't have to shield us anymore.

Third Spell's the Charm

Kane considered Hunt. "Why do you care about this death?"

"Apart from this being my club?" Hunt took a sip from his glass. "I'm looking for a killer vampire."

"Aren't all vampires killers?" I asked before I could think the wisdom of it. Hunt regarded me over the rim of his glass.

"Technically, yes."

"I'm not," Luca stated. "I've been ostracised for decades for not killing when I feed. I'm the only one who doesn't as far as I know. And I have no intentions to change."

Hunt sneered, but didn't say anything.

I amended my original question: "How does this killer vampire differ from others?"

"He leaves the bodies in the open."

Luca startled and Kane frowned. Apparently it was not done.

"Bodies? There's been more than one?" Luca asked.

"This was the fifth."

"And you've managed to keep them secret?" Kane asked.

Hunt nodded. "Each body has been left in one of my clubs. Hidden enough that they've only been found at the end of the night by the staff. Luckily, I have enough supernaturals working for me that they've known to call me instead of the police. I've handled the bodies and the memories of those humans who've witnessed them."

"Do you have any idea who it might be?" Kane asked. Hunt gave a pointed look at Luca, who growled.

"I did not do it!"

Hunt regarded him calmly from under his brows. "Then who?"

"How the fuck should I know? I don't have any contacts with vampires."

"Someone is issuing a challenge to me, and you're the only one who has a reason for it."

Luca huffed. "Hardly."

"What reason would Luca have to challenge you?" I asked.

"Like he said, he's been ostracised for decades."

"And I'm happy to be," Luca stated. "Most vampires are bastards."

Hunt's mouth quirked, amused now. "True…"

"So who else would want to challenge you?" Kane asked. "Who is more powerful than you?"

Hunt's eyes flashed in anger—literally, like lit by an inner light. It had to be a vampire thing.

Kane was unfazed. "There had to be a third vampire present, one that you couldn't sense, and that means they have to be more powerful than you."

Hunt growled, making small hairs in my body shoot up. Luca tensed too, but he leaned forward.

"How did you know to be here last night anyway?"

Hunt's jaw flexed, but he stopped growing. "The kills have happened every Saturday, one club at the time. This was the last of my clubs left. I intended to catch him red-handed. But there were too many people in the club and I couldn't get there in time. Then the body was out in the open and I had to deal with it, and couldn't go after them."

"If Luca was the only vampire you could sense, was he anywhere near Miss Peaches at the time he was killed?" I asked.

Third Spell's the Charm

"Yes. That's why I went there."

My gut tightened, but I pressed on. "Before or after we had left?"

"Well, you weren't there anymore when I found the body."

"Did you keep tabs on Luca the whole time?"

He frowned. "No. There were too many people around. But I definitely sensed him right before I found the body."

That was likely the moment we'd fled. Maybe Luca's panic had made his presence more pronounced. But it would make it more difficult to prove he didn't do it.

"So your last chance to catch the killer didn't work," Kane said, not mocking but stating a fact. "What do you intend to do next?"

Hunt spread his arms. "Wait for his next move. I can't believe this would be it just because I don't have any more clubs for him to kill in."

That didn't seem practical. "You can't just wait. You'll never catch him that way."

"You need to be proactive," Luca added, catching my idea immediately. "Like a detective hunting for clues."

He gave us a slow look. "I'm a CEO of a huge conglomerate. I don't have time to play detective."

"Maybe you could hire one," I suggested. "Someone who actually knows what they're doing."

He shook his head. "I can't use humans, because they wouldn't know what to look for even if I could tell them the truth about us. And if you're right and this vampire is more powerful than me, I can't send just any one of us after him either."

"You have to do something before this gets out of hands," Kane pointed out.

A slow sneer spread on Hunt's face. "Oh, I intend to. Luca, you will investigate this."

"Me?" Luca asked astonished. "What do I know about playing detective?"

"I suggest you learn. Fast."

"But surely you have people better suited for the job working for you."

"Not really. The vampires in my employ aren't terribly powerful. I can't send any of them after someone challenging me."

"But you can send me?"

Hunt shrugged. "You're powerful yourself. You'll manage. And you have mages helping you," he added, his upper lip curling with contempt.

"Leave my kind out of this," Kane stated. "This is an internal vampire matter."

"Are you sure? If I fall, and vampires are exposed, it's only a matter of time before humans learn about you too."

That silenced us.

"Let's say I accept your offer—" Luca began, and Hunt lifted a hand, interrupting him:

"Oh, it's not an offer. I'm still not convinced that you didn't do it. Either you find me the real killer, or I'll make a public example of you in lieu of them."

Luca tensed, but he continued gamely. "In order to investigate this properly, I'm going to need all the information you already have. How many bodies, who they were, and where they were found."

"And also a list of vampires powerful enough to take you, in London or outside," I added. Despite my better judgement, I was starting to warm up to this investigation. Finding the killer would be my last service for Miss Peaches.

Third Spell's the Charm

"Vampires don't exactly advertise on social media. I have no idea who is more powerful than me. Anything else?"

I could see he was amused by us, but it was better than angry. "Backup if we need to go after someone scary."

His amusement was wiped away. "If and when you find the person you deem is behind this, you'll leave the rest to me."

I was fine with that.

He tilted his head. "If that's all, I need to be elsewhere."

Luca and I all but shot up. Kane followed suit more calmly, reaching a hand over the table for Hunt to shake. He was braver than I. I wouldn't have touched Hunt if I were paid to.

Ronnie led us out through the staff area to the backyard. My entire body slumped in relief when the door closed behind us.

"That was scary."

"I told you he's dangerous," Luca said glumly.

"I thought you meant physical violence. Pressganging us to investigating deaths for him didn't cross my mind."

"You're not investigating anything," Luca stated. I straightened, incensed.

"Oh, come on. I can't let you do that alone. I was at the club too."

"Luca is right," Kane stated. "It could be dangerous."

I threw my arms up. "I know how to keep myself safe."

He gave me a slow look from under his raised brows. "Do I have to bring up how you recklessly faced a man with a gun?"

Jack had threatened to shoot me, but I resented the notion that I would've deliberately risked my life.

"That was necessary. Besides, nothing happened."

Nothing except Kane kissing me afterwards, but I tried not to think about that when he was around.

"Right…"

I ignored him and turned to Luca. "I'm good at spotting clues."

"Fine, but I'll do the legwork myself."

I could let him have that. For now.

KANE GAVE US A lift home, which we were grateful for, even though it had stopped raining. "Were you dining at the brasserie?" he asked when we were on our way. "I didn't notice you when we came in."

"No. Miss Peaches, the victim from last night, worked at the cabaret there. We went to see her boss for her contact information."

"Did they have it for you?"

"No," I sighed. "There had been some relationship drama and he didn't have the current address."

He glanced at me. "So why did you flee?"

I grimaced, but his attention was on the traffic. "Luca is afraid of Hunt, and he panicked."

"Hey!"

I glanced at Luca over the backrest. "You are."

"Well, can you blame me?"

I couldn't.

Kane shook his head. "Morgan was so intrigued by it that we had to abandon our dinner before it even arrived to pursue you."

Third Spell's the Charm

"I told you, vampires are all about the hunt," Luca said, triumphant, but I ignored him for the other part of Kane's answer.

"You didn't get to eat?" Embarrassed flush swept through me. "Would you like to come to dine over our place?"

Giselle always made plenty of food.

Kane gave me a warm smile. "Thank you, I'd love to."

Giselle was happy to see Kane and immediately set a plate for him. Since the dinner was ready, we sat down and filled our plates.

Amber picked up her utensils. "Did you find the next of kin of the victim?"

"No, but we have his legal name, and I can do a search after dinner," Luca told her. "And we know what happened to the body."

The women perked, expectant, and Luca leaned closer.

"Morgan Hunt moved it away."

"Did he kill her?" Giselle asked, paling.

"Not according to him." I reached for the water pitcher and poured myself some. "But he's convinced Luca did."

"He's making me investigate."

"Why?" Amber asked.

Luca placed his glass in front of me and I poured him a glass too. "It's his club. He has several of them and the vampire has been leaving bodies in all of them. He wants me to find out who's challenging him."

"And I'm helping," I added.

"If someone is moving against Hunt, that'll spell trouble for all of us," Kane said. Amber nodded, her face grim.

"Do you think it's someone more powerful than him or only more foolish?"

Kane rested his knife and fork against the plate and gave her a self-deprecating look. "Let's hope for more foolish. I can't deal with another power struggle just yet."

Julius Blackhart, a mage at the level of an archmage, had tried to take the Mages' Council from Kane, and to become a warlock by sacrificing Giselle. We had won, but only barely, and he was roaming free somewhere. Amber now led the council, and Kane was studying to become an archmage so that we'd be better prepared when Blackhart returned.

We talked about other issues for the rest of the dinner. We'd almost finished when Kane tilted his head and gave me a puzzled look.

"Is there something new about you, Phoebe?"

Six

I'D FORGOTTEN ABOUT THE HORRID fringe. Trust him to notice it when he usually didn't pay any attention. I groaned, annoyed.

"Yes. I have bangs now."

He lifted his brows. "You don't sound happy about it. Why did you cut it?"

"Out of necessity."

I would've left it at that, but Giselle laughed. "She set her hair on fire practicing a spell."

Kane looked delighted. "You've advanced to a fire spell already?"

"No," I groaned, pressing my face in my hands in embarrassment. "It was the water spell."

He was so quiet I risked lifting my face. He was biting his lips, desperately trying not to laugh, making an honest to God dimple appear on his cheek. I'd never noticed it before.

Then again, he was seldom shaken from his lofty state quite this thoroughly.

He inhaled deeply, controlling his mirth, but his eyes were twinkling. "I see. Well, you'll get the hang of it eventually."

I didn't share his optimism.

We rose from the table and settled on the comfier chairs in the living room to have tea. Luca took out his phone to search for Sam Selby. He frowned, annoyed.

"I can't find a single Sam Selby that matches the age profile of Miss Peaches, or who even lives in London."

I leaned over to look too, as if that would make a difference. "Do you think it's an assumed name?"

"Could be. Maybe his family has thrown him out or something and he's changed his name."

Sadness filled me for the notion that the vibrant Miss Peaches would have been hiding such an unhappy past. "Try Miss Peaches. Performers are bound to have an online presence."

There was an instant hit. "Definitely her."

Her Instagram account had dozens if not hundreds of photos of her in various outfits, with different makeups and wigs, on stage and off—and not a single one out of drag. She looked vibrant and happy, but she was alone in most of the pictures, only some of the stage photos had other people in them. Not one was of a romantic partner, and there was no one tagged as family.

Luca shook his head. "This doesn't really help us to find where she was staying or who would know more about her next of kin."

"Is there any kind of spell we could try?" I asked hopefully. Amber pursed her lips, thinking.

"What are you trying to do?"

"To find out where Miss Peaches was staying."

Kane gave it a thought too. "We'd need an item that belonged to her."

"I have the calling card," Luca said, showing it to Kane.

Third Spell's the Charm

"That's not terribly personal, but there's no harm trying."

He gave a questioning look at Amber and Giselle, who were eager to try their hands at it.

We climbed into the attic. Amber fetched a book about protective circles, located the correct one and began to draw it on the polished floor. A pattern this complicated couldn't exactly be memorised and one had to be careful not to make mistakes with them. Otherwise the outcome of the spell could change, or it might fail to take completely.

"When will I learn to draw these?" I asked curiously, watching her work.

She gave me a pointed look. "Once you've mastered the basic element spells."

I'd been afraid she'd say that.

When she was done, the mages went through the spell together, each memorising their part in it with seeming ease, even though it was long and complicated.

Giselle fetched a detailed map of London from one of the shelves lining the room and spread it on the floor. Luca gave her the card and she placed it on the map. Then the mages took their spots on the pattern.

"Phoebe, you should pay close attention to what we do, especially the rhythm of the spell," Amber instructed me. I had intended to follow the spell closely anyway, but the rhythm wouldn't have occurred to me.

Large spells were complicated.

Then they began. The first part of any spell was always about gathering energy. According to Amber and Giselle, it came from nature, which had been somewhat of a relief to me, as I'd feared it might come from dark forces or something.

The energy was captured in the pattern and made to multiply. The more energy a spell needed, the more complicated the pattern and the longer it took to multiply. But it spared the mage from draining themselves in the process.

This one took quite a while to build. I could feel it pressing against me. Kane's hair was billowing as if in a storm. This was the most straining part of the spell for mages. If they weren't each doing their part, one of them might end up doing more than they had strength for, which could be dangerous. At the very least, the spell might collapse.

When the energy had built enough, they began the actual incantation, saying the words firmly at the same time. I could feel the spell take as the energy drained from the pattern towards the centre where the card was. It began to float wildly, and then abruptly settled on the map, balancing on one corner to point the exact location.

The mages looked satisfied. Tired, but satisfied. Giselle stepped out of the circle and headed downstairs. "I'll make tea." It would be restorative for the mages, and something to help me sleep.

Amber wrote down the address the card had pointed to. "I don't know if this is where Miss Peaches was living, but the card has definitely been there."

It was a start.

Luca took the note, smiling. "Thank you. We'll go check it tomorrow. It's too late to go tonight."

Satisfied, we all headed back to kitchen for Giselle's excellent tea.

MONDAY MORNING BROKE as rainy as the previous days had been. It was good news for Luca, who could venture outside during the day, but it meant a miserable, damp commute for me in a Tube car that smelled like a wet dog.

The short walk from Bond Street Station to Kane's Arts and Antiques on the north side of Oxford Street was a struggle. Wind was picking up, tugging my umbrella and throwing rain on me despite my efforts to shield myself.

The shop was located on a narrow pedestrian court, with cafés and clothes shops surrounding it on all sides. My favourite café was right across the court from the shop, and I glanced at it wistfully. I could've used their excellent coffee and blueberry muffin this morning, but I didn't feel like queueing with a bunch of wet people, so I abstained.

The antique shop occupied a small, elegant showroom with dark walls and hardwood floor, mahogany shelves and glass display cases filled with all manner of portable antiques, from snuff boxes and miniatures to statuettes and table lamps.

Adjoined to the shop was a larger space where we held art exhibitions and auctions that were very popular. We would hold one on Saturday of rare maps and prints from the fifteenth to the seventeenth centuries. They were generating a lot of interest and we were anticipating a roaring success.

It was quite a coup really. Sotheby's, where I had trained auctioneering, and other big auction houses would've wanted to auction them. They couldn't understand why our small shop was given the honour.

Little did they know that the seller was a mage friend of Kane's who insisted on us selling his treasure. The collection held books and prints on magic too, but those would be sold privately.

The items on the public auction were invaluable, and insurance for showcasing them would've been astronomical if they'd been stored in the shop. They were therefore held in a bank vault until the auction, with only an online catalogue for buyers to see.

They would arrive on Saturday morning, and we'd hired private security for the day to appease the insurance company. We weren't worried though. Kane would ward the room so that no one could steal anything.

Not that we could tell that to the insurance company.

Like every morning, I was the first to arrive. The shop was closed on Mondays and Mrs Walsh who manned it had a day off. It was dark except for the security light on the shop window. Out of habit, I glanced in, but it was empty. The windows of the exhibition space were covered up while we prepared the room for the auction.

The offices were above the shop, and they were accessed through their own door next to the shop. I entered to the tiny space that had barely enough room for a door to the shop and narrow stairs up. I disabled the alarm, picked up the mail, straightened—and screeched in fright, when a man appeared in the doorway to the shop.

"I'm sorry. I didn't mean to frighten you," Kane said remorsefully, crouching to collect the mail I'd scattered all over.

I slumped against the front door, hand over my mouth, trying to get my breathing to calm.

"You're not usually here at this hour," I managed to say. He arrived promptly at nine every morning, giving me time to go through the morning mail and brew his tea. "And I just looked through the shop window and it was empty."

"I was in the exhibition room."

Third Spell's the Charm

"Did the new display finally arrive?" I asked, pushing myself upright, my breathing calming.

Since people weren't allowed to touch the maps and they would be kept in their cases, we'd purchased a 4K display to present the items in detail for the prospective buyers.

He shook his head. "Not yet. But I'm keeping my fingers crossed for later this morning like they promised."

"They promised it for last Monday morning," I said dryly. I wasn't panicking yet, but we needed the systems up and running well before Saturday so that we could test them.

This was in my purview as Kane's assistant. I handled the mail and sundry, and all the details that went into a good auction. In fact, everything he found mystifying and/or boring were mine to handle. He travelled the country, evaluating items and making finds for the shop. He had a good nose for antiques, and often found interesting items.

"What brings you here this early, then?"

"Since the exhibition space is empty, I thought we could look into why your water spell doesn't behave as it ought to," Kane said.

He held the door to the shop open for me. I wasn't in a spellcasting frame of mind, and I had a ton of work waiting for me upstairs, but I went in. If your almost-archmage of a boss decides to teach you how to properly cast a water spell, you pay attention.

I left my wet umbrella in the umbrella stand by the shop door, and my bag and scarf on the display counter, and followed Kane to the gallery.

It was a rectangular room that had been painted deep wine red for the upcoming auction, with print copies of some of the maps hung on them. Folding chairs were waiting in piles by one wall, and the display cases were at the back wall, ready to be spread to their places once the real merchandise arrived.

The hardwood floor was currently empty, but it wasn't bare. Kane had drawn three interconnecting circles on it, two large enough to fit a person and a small one holding a shallow earthenware bowl.

"These larger circles are for protection," he explained. "The small one is for focusing magic. See how the symbols differ?"

I had a degree in art history and a good eye for patterns, so I was able to spot the differences in the curling figures easily.

"But it's me I keep igniting. How will it help if I'm inside the circle?"

He smiled, pleased for my question, with no hint of the mirth of yesterday. "This is a special circle, inside which it's impossible for a spell to take. The smaller one should draw it instead."

"And if it doesn't?"

He glanced up. "Then we'd best hope the sprinkler system works."

Funny.

We settled down on the floor, each in our own circle. My tight jeans and boots weren't suited for it, and I had some trouble finding a comfortable position. Kane, in his customary three-piece today, didn't seem to have a similar problem.

I should've worn a skirt.

"Let's start with calming our minds," he said.

"I don't think that's happening," I confessed. "Having you here rather makes me nervous."

Third Spell's the Charm

A corner of his mouth quirked, and his blue eyes were warm. "This will not go on your job evaluation."

"Good to know." I didn't add that I needed to impress him, and knowing that the opposite would happen didn't help.

Closing my eyes so that I could imagine he wasn't here, I inhaled deeply. The subtle, expensive scent he wore reached my noise, distracting me again.

I ignored it the best I could and calmed my mind. Then I reached for the spark inside me. Once I had it, I did the correct hand gestures and said the incantation aloud.

I opened my eyes. "Did it work?"

He tilted his head, studying the bowl. "Good news is, you didn't burn your hair this time round. But you didn't conjure water either."

My shoulders slumped. "It's somehow even worse."

"Let's try with this." He tore a piece of paper from the pile of mail he'd carried in with him, and put it on the bowl. "Cast it again."

I took the same steps as earlier. This time, I sensed the spell take—and smelled burning paper. I opened my eyes just in time to see the piece of paper turn to ash in the bowl.

"Bummer."

Kane pursed his lips. "Fascinating. Let's try a different spell. This one requires a bit more energy. You clearly have some extra, because everything else seems to be in order."

That was good to hear at least.

"It's a wind spell for moving air. This is the incantation."

He recited the words, a simple enough spell that I had no trouble repeating and memorising. Then followed the gestures that were also simple. Once he deemed that I could make them correctly, he took out a feather from his pocket, as if it were a perfectly normal thing to carry around. He put the feather in the bowl.

"You don't have to direct the spell, the circles will do that. All you have to do is cast the spell and the feather will fly."

Nervous again, I concentrated, rehearsing the elements of the spell in my head. I kept my eyes open this time, as closing them clearly made no difference. Then I cast the spell.

The feather burst into flame.

Kane scratched his brow, staring at the smelly remains in disbelief. "Well, that didn't work."

Unshed tears tightened my throat. "I'll never be a mage."

He gave me a reassuring look. "You already are. It's something inside you." His lips quirked. "Whether you'll be a great spellcaster remains to be seen. But it's early days and you're older than people usually are when they start. Keep at it, and you'll get there in the end."

"Shall I try again?"

"Not today. It's exhausting when you're a beginner, and we have actual work to do."

He got up in a sinuous motion, but when I tried the same my legs wouldn't obey. Part of it was the uncomfortable position I'd been sitting in, but mostly it was having drained all my energy.

"Here, let me help."

He offered me a hand and pulled me up easily. My legs held, but my head twirled. He wrapped an arm around my shoulders, and I leaned my forehead against his chest, listening to his steady heartbeat until the dizziness passed.

"Let's get you upstairs. I'll make you tea," Kane said, concerned. I shot him an alarmed look.

"I'm not dead. I'll make tea."

He grinned. "I think I can manage it this once."

Turned out, Kane could brew an excellent cup. No wonder he was so fussy about his tea. Revived by it, I set out to handle the day's work while Kane locked himself into his office.

In other words, back to business as usual.

At some point, I went back downstairs and mopped the chalk circles off the floor. It wouldn't do for Mrs Walsh to pop in on her day off and see them. She'd give her notice at once, and we wouldn't easily find such a competent replacement.

The TV display still wasn't delivered by the end of the business day

Seven

LUCA ARRIVED AS I WAS gathering my things at the end of the day. He was wrapped up for the weather, carrying an umbrella against the rain and excess light, and he looked happier than in ages, despite the errand we were about to run.

"It's so wonderful to be out and about at the same time other people are," he told me.

Kane exited his office on his way home. He gave Luca a baffled look and then glanced at his wristwatch—a Heuer Carrera from the 1960s he had purchased in an auction a while back and was excessively proud of—as if to check how late it was if Luca was out and about.

His brow cleared when it turned out to be his usual time to leave. "Are you two headed to talk with whoever lives at the location the spell indicated?"

"Yes. The faster we find out who to inform about Miss Peaches's death, the better," I said with a sigh. I wasn't looking forward to the task, but it had to be done.

"It's not like Hunt will handle it," Luca added dryly.

"Do you want me to come with you?" Kane asked. A part of me wanted to say yes, but Luca shook his head before I managed to open my mouth.

"We'll manage. We don't know if there's even anyone home."

"Let me give you a lift, then."

Luca shook his head again. "Thanks, but we'll walk."

"Walk?" I exclaimed. "In this weather? That's over two miles."

He grinned. "It's not even raining anymore. And I desperately want to be outdoors during the daylight."

When he put it like that, I couldn't refuse. I was wearing good boots and I could skip jogging tonight.

It was a forty-five-minute walk south through Central London and across the Thames to Waterloo Station. I was seldom around here during the day, and I studied the familiar landmarks with interest. Crossing Trafalgar Square, I spotted a large poster of a Vermeer exhibition at the National Gallery that I'd meant to see. It would end on Sunday, so I'd best hurry up.

"Do we have time to see that?"

"How about on our way back," he suggested. "If we have energy."

I wouldn't count on it, but I didn't argue. The journey was fun enough. Luca was a great companion with his delight of daylight, even though the day was overcast. He told funny anecdotes about the landmarks as we passed them, and people who were long gone. Even the light drizzle that began when we crossed the river didn't dampen his joy.

Our destination was on the east side of Waterloo Station, on a narrow, winding street that was positively Dickensian. Each side of the street was a continuous row of a two-storey, brown-brick workers' terrace from the nineteenth century, with doors straight to the pavement and no trimmings whatsoever to separate one house from

Third Spell's the Charm

the other, or to offer relief from the bleakness. There were no flower arrangements or anything green growing there. Even with the smog soot washed off the walls, and fresh paint on the doors and small-paned window frames, it still looked dreary. The street probably featured in every period drama on TV.

Judging by the cars parked on the street, however, you couldn't get a house here with a railway worker's salary anymore—or even a middleclass one.

"It's number eleven," Luca said, and we checked the numbers on the doors until we found the correct one, painted bright red. I made to knock on the door, when Luca halted me, his head cocked to the side as if he was listening to something.

"I ... think there's a vampire inside."

My heart jumped. "The killer?"

"I have no idea."

We exchanged worried glances. "Should we ... call backup?"

"Hunt?" He shuddered. "I fear him more."

I kind of did too, but if we'd inadvertently stumbled upon the killer, Hunt needed to know. But before I could say so, the door was yanked open, startling us both. I might have shrieked a little.

"What do you want?" the man on the doorstep demanded, only to pause, baffled, his eyes narrowing as he studied Luca. "Is it...?"

"Luca Marlow," Luca provided smoothly, recovering from the man's sudden appearance. "And you are...?"

"Adam Finch."

The men nodded at each other and smiled like they were old school chums, not best of friends but happy to see each other after all these years. I stared at them, bemused.

"Do you know each other?"

Luca smiled. "Let's say we've known each other as our previous selves."

That explained the odd introductions.

"What brings you here so unexpectedly?" Finch asked. He was an ordinary looking man seemingly in his mid-thirties, but being a vampire, who knew how old he was. His hair was cut neatly, and he was wearing business casual, as if he'd just come home from work. I wondered if he was powerful enough to work outside home during the day.

Luca grimaced. "It's a delicate business. May we come in?"

He let us in, and I looked around with shameless curiosity. "I've never been into one of these houses."

The door opened to a cramped hallway, most of which was taken by steep and narrow stairs up. On one side was a small parlour and on the other an equally small dining room, each with a window facing the street. I surmised the kitchen was at the back, but the door there was closed.

The house was in a beautiful condition, the wooden floor polished and the walls covered with reproductions of Victorian wallpapers the house most likely hadn't originally come with, having been built for people who couldn't afford them. The furniture was a mixture of antique and retro pieces that made my fingers itch to look closer.

Finch glanced around as he gestured us to precede him to the parlour. "I've lived here about a decade. The previous owner fixed the place, but the furniture is mine."

"It looks wonderful."

Luca gave me a pointed look. "We're not here to talk about décor."

Nodding, I took a seat on an elegant Chippendale chair. "Sorry."

"What is it?" Finch asked curiously. "You don't usually seek out other vampires."

"And I wouldn't have done so now if I hadn't been forced to by Morgan Hunt."

Finch made a face. "What did you do?"

"I was in the wrong place at the wrong time." Luca sighed. "A vampire's been killing humans and leaving them in nightclubs Hunt owns."

"Hunt owns nightclubs?" Finch exclaimed, and Luca dipped his chin in the affirmative.

"I was surprised too. But someone's clearly gone through the trouble to learn everything about Hunt's businesses, because he's left a body in each of his five clubs. Last one was this Saturday."

Luca glanced down, gathering himself, or trying to come up with a way to approach this.

"Do you know a drag performer named Miss Peaches? Sam Selby?"

A faint blush rose to Finch's cheeks. "Maybe. Why?"

My stomach clenched in sudden horror. "Are you the ex-boyfriend?"

The blush deepened. "We had a huge row, yes, and he moved out, but I'm sure we'll get past it."

Luca and I exchanged stricken glances. "Does ... did you tell him you're a vampire?" he asked. Finch lifted hands in front of him, as if rejecting the mere notion.

"Of course not. That's why we were fighting. I couldn't participate in everything he wanted to do, and I didn't have a good explanation for why I stayed home, especially on nice, sunny summer days. There are only so many times I can mesmerise a person before it stops having an effect." He grimaced. "I don't feel it's right to mesmerise a person you love."

I could understand that.

"Were you together for a long time?" I asked, fighting tears.

"No, only since ... February. Things started to go sour during the summer, and then last month he moved out." He gave us a sharp look. "Why are you asking about him?"

I shot a beseeching look at Luca, who sighed. "I'm sorry, but Miss Peaches, Sam, was the vampire's latest victim."

Finch blinked, uncomprehending. "What are you saying?"

"He's dead."

Adam's face turned to stone. A low growl made his voice rumble. "Who?"

"We have no idea. We're trying to investigate, but we only started."

His growl grew louder, making the small hairs in my neck rise. "I want the name the moment you find out."

Luca nodded. "Absolutely, but Hunt will get it first."

"He had better be fast, then, to beat me to it." He controlled his anger with effort, and I sighed in relief when the pressure on me eased. It wasn't as bad as Hunt's, but it was unnerving.

He shook his head, deflating. "How did you find me anyway?"

"Magic," I said. "We met Miss Peaches at the club the night she died, and she gave us her calling card. We spoke to her boss, but he didn't know where she was currently

Third Spell's the Charm

staying, so we asked some mages to perform a locating spell with the card. It led us here."

"Maxim didn't know where she was staying?" He sounded incredulous. "Why didn't he send you directly here, then?"

"Apparently he didn't know who you were or have the address."

Finch snorted. "Right..." He rubbed his face with both hands, looking tired all of a sudden. "What are you going to do next?"

Luca spread his arms. "Everything we can possibly think of. Because if we don't solve this Hunt will pin it on me. And I won't survive that."

It had turned dark by the time we exited Finch's house, so we took the Tube home. I was more tired than the walking would merit, the visit having drained me, and I didn't even suggest we go to the National Gallery.

We went in through the shop. It was a charming place that sold herbal tea and remedies, spell books, healing crystals, and other harmless items anyone could buy. It also had a couple of small tables for those who wished to have a cup of tea. However, for those in the know, the shop also sold professional ingredients that were used in actual spells.

Amber handed us a packet as we passed the cashier's desk at the back of the shop on our way to the stairs. "Hunt sent this."

"Physical files?" Luca asked, baffled, as he took the packet. "Has the man not heard of cloud services?"

"He's an old vampire," I said as we headed upstairs. "He probably makes notes on paper."

"I'm an old vampire, and I know how to use digital services," he said dryly.

"Maybe you're special," I quipped, making him laugh.

Dinner wasn't ready yet, so we settled on the sofa and Luca opened the packet. Griselda came to greet us, and I picked her up, watching Luca pull out four thin files and spread them on the coffee table in front of us. It wasn't much to work on.

"These are organised by date," he said, opening the first one.

He took out a photo—not of a dead body, to my relief—of a twenty-something man with blond hair and earnest eyes, and gave the file a quick read.

"Erich Kessler, twenty-two, a German exchange student at LSE. According to Hunt's notes, he had the body returned to Germany with an official report that Kessler had OD'd in a club. Not Hunt's. LSE was informed of the same."

That was a neat solution.

"Is there anything useful?"

He shook his head. "That's all there is."

He picked another file and took out a photo of a pretty but tired-looking woman in her early thirties with short-cropped black hair. "Sherry Beck, thirty-two. A nurse at St Thomas's Hospital. She was found in a club near the hospital, so maybe she'd gone there alone after an evening shift."

I didn't know much about nursing, but I found it incredible one would have energy to go clubbing after work. Maybe it had helped her unwind.

"Did she have family?"

"A boyfriend, no children. Hunt made that one look like a knife attack outside Waterloo Station. There was

Third Spell's the Charm

some ado about it in the papers, but no suspicious questions have been asked."

"Finch lives near Waterloo Station," I noted, and he nodded, looking grim.

"I wouldn't put it past him to have lied to us."

"His grief seemed genuine." I'd certainly been moved by it, but not so Luca.

"He's an old vampire. He has learned to pretend."

"Old enough to have learned how not to be detected by other vampires?"

He gave me a sharp look. "I have no idea. Age isn't talked about among our kind. But I did detect him at his home."

I petted Griselda, mulling it over. "Maybe it's something he can turn on and off, and he'd turned it off at home."

"Could be. But let's check the rest before we make any conclusions."

The third photo was of a man in his late twenties with very dark brown skin, dressed in traditional Nigerian clothes. He was looking at the camera with a wide smile.

"Chinwe Okafor, twenty-nine, a Nigerian tourist visiting relatives in London. According to his last Facebook post, he wanted to check out the London nightlife and apparently went alone. Hunt made it look like a traffic accident."

"Busy man."

Luca tilted his head in acknowledgement. "It's what we most often do with our victims, stage a believable scenario for the death so that there won't be questions asked. Saves us from altering too many memories."

Last photo was a Vietnamese girl who looked barely old enough to go clubbing. "Phan Yên Thu, twenty years old. She went to one of Hunt's clubs on a date, but according to her social media post the guy was a jerk, so she dumped him and left for home. Only she never left the club. Hunt staged her body to have fallen under a train. Her family is devastated and demanded an inquiry, but the surveillance footage appeared to show it was an accident."

I shook my head, amazed. "Hunt can arrange that but not share these files electronically?"

Luca shrugged. "Maybe he has people for doctoring footage, and then he alters their memories."

That made sense. I studied the photos Luca had spread on the table, petting Griselda as I tried to think. "Do any of the victims matter?" I blushed, embarrassed. "I mean, obviously they matter to their families. But they seem so random."

Luca nodded. "The places matter, not the people. The killer is after Hunt, not whoever he killed. But it kind of looks like he's gone out of his way to have as diverse set of victims as possible."

"He's taken an oddly roundabout way to attack Hunt," I mused, trying to figure out connections with the victims and finding nothing else than Hunt's clubs.

"He's a vampire. He likes to play before the killing strike."

The victims clearly weren't the key, so we needed a different approach. "What could be his motive?"

He shrugged. "Who knows with vampires that old? Could be a grudge over seating arrangements at a dinner in 1812 or something as trivial, or it could be boredom. Or it could be a genuine play for removing Hunt and taking his place."

Third Spell's the Charm

We stared at the photos some more, but they yielded no insights.

Luca eventually sighed, rubbing his face. "I have no idea how to conduct an investigation like this."

"Didn't you used to study law?"

He gave me a slow look. "That was a century ago. And I wasn't the most diligent student. I preferred absinthe parties to studies. How do you think I ended up as a vampire?"

"By going clubbing alone?" I guessed. He made a gun with his thumb and forefinger and pointed it at me.

"Bingo."

My gut tightened. "Is this personal to you?"

"It was a long time ago," he said, brushing my concern away. "I'm not going to have panic attacks or bouts of melancholy over this."

I patted his knee. "Good to know. But in case you do, I'm here for you."

"Thanks."

We stared at the papers again in silence. They didn't mysteriously reveal their secrets or offer any clues that we could've followed this time round either.

"Why the nightclubs?" I finally asked. Luca gave me a puzzled look.

"Because Hunt owns them?"

"But he owns a huge conglomerate that would've made a much more impressive target, and Ronnie said no one really knows these clubs belong to Hunt. Finch didn't know it."

"Maybe the vampire wants to show that they've done their homework and found hidden things about Hunt," Luca suggested.

"And these deaths were just to get his attention?"

"Or an opening salvo."

"Some opening, five deaths."

Luca grimaced. "Not that I'm defending them, but for old vampires, human life is cheap. He probably thinks it a perfectly reasonable way to make his move against Hunt. And Hunt isn't bothered by the bodies either, only about how it'll reflect on his businesses if they're found on his premises."

I nodded. "If this was just the opening, what can we expect next?"

"Anything, really."

"More deaths?"

"Most likely."

Wonderful.

"I don't think we get anywhere by guessing what the vampire might be after or do next," I said, heaving such a deep sigh that it disturbed Griselda, who had been sleeping on my lap. She got up and jumped down, disappearing under the furniture.

Luca drummed the table. "Maybe there's surveillance footage from the clubs that I could go through to see if there are any familiar faces."

"Maybe Hunt has done that already?"

"I doubt it. It's time consuming. But I have great software for it, same as the police use."

"Where did you get that?"

He grinned. "I have my ways."

Our research came to an end when Giselle ordered us to set the table. "Ashley is at work, so one place less tonight."

Amber arrived from the shop and we sat down to enjoy the dinner. "Have you made any progress with the case?" she asked. Luca nodded.

Third Spell's the Charm

"We learned that Miss Peaches's ex-boyfriend was a vampire named Adam Finch. I used to know him with a different name."

"They'd broken up because he couldn't tell her he's a vampire," I added. Tears sprang to my eyes. "She said in the queue she'd always wanted to meet a vampire. If only she'd known…"

We concentrated on our dinner in silence. Amber eventually broke the silence. "Do you want to practice spell casting tonight, Phoebe?"

"Kane taught me the wind spell today," I told her, perking. She smiled.

"And did you set your hair in fire?"

"No…" She kept staring at me, so I gave in. "It was the feather."

Eight

THERE WAS A HUGE RECTANGULAR parcel waiting outside the shop door when I reached Kane's Arts and Antiques the next morning. The office door was for deliveries and no one just left the parcels outside without signing off on them.

Baffled, I went to look—and almost growled like Luca and Ashley at their best. It was the TV. How the hell was I supposed to get it indoors all by myself?

I was saved by Mrs Walsh, who arrived unusually early. She was in her fifties, a mother of three grown sons, and shorter than me by half a head without the death-defying heels she always wore with her elegant—and expensive—designer clothing. Chanel today.

She raised a carefully painted brow. "Is that the TV we've been waiting for since last week?"

"Yes. They left it here."

"That's rude. Hang on, I'll go switch off the alarm."

Soon she had the door to the shop open and together we carried the large box inside. It wasn't as heavy as I'd believed, but it was difficult to handle because of its size. We got it into the exhibition space without incident, and unboxed the TV.

"Now we'll just have to mount it," Mrs Walsh noted.

I eyed the stand hanging from the ceiling with misgivings. I was a good assistant, but there were limits to my abilities. Climbing on a ladder lugging a huge TV was definitely outside my skillset.

"Maybe we should wait until Mr Kane arrives," Mrs Walsh suggested, following my gaze. I gave her a dubious look and she smiled. "Or I'll ask one of my sons to drop by later."

That would be more helpful.

She began to gather the remains of the box and halted. "Why is there a chalk line on the floor?"

My stomach tightened. I hadn't cleaned up as thoroughly as I hoped after our little practice session the previous morning. "We ... wanted to check that there was enough room for all the display cases and the chairs, but didn't want to move them around, so we used chalk."

I didn't like lying to her, but the truth truly was too much.

She pursed her lips. "You should be more thorough cleaning up."

I most assuredly would be.

We were still trying to figure out how to mount the TV when Kane walked in. "Why are you here? There was no tea." Then he took in what we were doing. "Did the TV finally arrive? Does it work?"

We hadn't even come to think to check. I plugged it in, and Mrs Walsh switched it on, but nothing happened. We double-checked the cables and the remote batteries, but there was no change. Good thing we hadn't mounted the thing first.

Kane's brows furrowed. "I'll call the shop."

Third Spell's the Charm

I was about to say I'd handle it when a man spoke behind us.

"Maybe I can be of assistance?"

We pivoted to the voice, startled for the unexpected presence, as the shop was officially closed. Hunt was standing at the opening between the shop and the exhibition space, calm and cool in his business suit, auburn hair neatly combed back.

"The conference rooms at my company's premises received new displays yesterday. Some of them are still in their transportation packages. You can borrow one."

I'm sure there was a saying about looking a vampire's gift in the mouth—or about vampire's mouths and gifts—but it was the easiest solution for the auction.

Kane nodded. "Thank you. Perhaps I can be of assistance in return?"

Translation: *What do you want for it, and it had better not be blood.*

Hunt made an elegant gesture with his hand, drawing attention to his long fingers. "How about a first look into the other items you're selling for Mr Mead?"

I couldn't fathom what a vampire would do with spell books, grimoires, and other magic related items, but the overly casual way he asked indicated he was extremely interested.

Kane nodded. "I have them in my office safe." He gestured at Hunt to precede him out of the room. Since I wasn't needed at the shop, I followed them.

In Kane's office, I asked if the men wanted tea, but both declined. I could've used some myself, but there was no point brewing a pot just for myself.

I was about to leave them to their negotiations when Hunt shot me a piercing look. "Did you find the killer yesterday?"

I pulled back. "How did you know we went to look?"

"I know everything," he stated. "Well?"

I sat gingerly on the edge of the sofa at the side of the room. "We went to find the next of kin of Miss Peaches, or Sam Shelby as he was known off-stage. Turned out, the spell led us to a vampire named Adam Finch who was his ex-boyfriend."

His eyes sharpened. "I know who he is. Is he the killer?"

"Our news came as a shock to him. He seemed genuinely grieved for the death."

"*Could* he have been the killer?"

I made a vague gesture. "I have no idea, but Luca could sense him through the door, so maybe he's not powerful enough to hide what he is."

"Maybe. I'll have to visit him." He shook himself and turned to Kane. "Now, about those items…"

"Is there anything particular you'd be interested in?" Kane asked, smoothly changing to a salesman tone.

"I'll let you know when I see it."

Hunt might be an old vampire, but he was just like all the clients we had, pretending disinterest in the hopes that we wouldn't up the price.

The safe was a huge walk-in, accessed through a closet in Kane's office. It had been there already when he had acquired the place, and was one of the prime reasons he had.

Kane fetched a large box and placed it on the coffee table in front of the sofa. Hunt moved to sit next to me, and I had to fight not to pull away.

Third Spell's the Charm

Kane lifted the items from the box one by one, and I kept an eye on Hunt to see which one caught his interest. It was one of the last items, an ordinary looking book from maybe the eighteenth century, printed, not a manuscript. Hunt was good at keeping his face disinterested, but the flash in his eyes was unmistakeable.

"How much for the lot?" Hunt asked when Kane had lifted out the last item. Kane gave him a steady look.

"I'm not selling it to you in bulk. The books are important to mages, and potentially dangerous in the hands of anyone else."

"I'm perfectly capable of performing magic."

"That's what I'm afraid of," my boss said dryly.

Hunt came as close to rolling his eyes as he was able. "Fine, which are the items you're absolutely not going to let me touch?"

Kane studied the items on the low table with sharpness he only reserved for antiques. Then he selected most of the oldest books, an ancient chart that I had no idea what it was used for, and a couple of random-looking items, and put them back in the box.

Two books, including the one Hunt wanted, remained, with a star chart that I rather fancied myself if I could've afforded it, and some ancient but not terribly valuable items used in potion making, like a stone mortar and pestle that had been used so much there were deep grooves in the stone.

Hunt barely glanced at them. "How much for this lot, then?"

"A hundred thousand pounds," Kane stated with a straight face. Hunt inhaled a snort.

"Don't be absurd. I wouldn't have paid that much even with the other items. I'll give you five thousand for it."

While the men settled for negotiating the price, I tried to look closer at the book Hunt wanted without him noticing. Apart from the age, it didn't look remarkable; it was a scholarly study of folklore. The author, Bernard Bishop, wasn't anyone I'd ever heard of. He was likely one of the dozens of gentleman scholars who'd spent their abundant spare time writing and publishing books about their particular interest that no one had ever read.

Yet there had to be something about the book, because Hunt wanted it.

After a heated negotiation, Hunt agreed to pay twelve thousand. It was an excellent price for the items; five thousand would've been an overkill. I barely managed to contain my excitement, but Kane looked mildly displeased and not merely for form.

I stood up, glad for the excuse to put some distance between Hunt and me, and leaned to gather the items. "I'll wrap these up for you. Do you want to take them with you, or shall I have them delivered?"

"I'll take these immediately," Hunt stated, picking up the books before I had the chance. "You can bring the rest to my house at eight this evening with Luca. He knows the address. Don't be late."

He shook hands with Kane and was out of the door in a few long strides, leaving me to stare after him in dismay. I did not want to go to his home. But since I couldn't refuse—and not merely because he wasn't here to refuse to anymore—I carried the items to the shop where Mrs Walsh and I wrapped them carefully in silk paper and placed them in a paper bag with our shop's name on it.

Third Spell's the Charm

Back at my desk, I powered up my computer, late to start the day's tasks. But instead of handling them, I started a search for the book Hunt had wanted.

London had several sellers of rare and antique books, but none of them had the book in their online catalogues. That didn't necessarily mean they didn't have it in their collections, but I wasn't feeling hopeful.

Instead, I turned to the British Library, which produced an immediate result. They even had a helpful link to an online database of eighteenth-century books. For an astronomical yearly subscription price that few universities were willing to pay, one could read and download files of every book they'd scanned. But one download was free, and that was all I needed.

The pdf-file securely downloaded to my laptop, I opened it. It was poor quality, indicating that the book it had been scanned from was badly worn—unlike the pristine copy we'd just sold to Hunt. The table of contents instantly revealed why he had wanted it.

The Fantastical Creatures of British Islands, and How to Protect One From Them was a book about the supernatural creatures of Britain. A couple of months ago I would've believed that the author was an eccentric who had been taken by his imagination. But now I knew that at least some of the creatures named in the table of contents were real, so who was to say that elves and pixies and what have you the book also listed weren't.

I badly wanted to read everything the author had written about everything, but I flipped the file to the chapter on vampires—and my heart stopped in shock.

The chapter opened with an etching of a portrait of an aristocratic man in the finery of the eighteenth century: an embroidered coat with a satin waistcoat, shirt with lace ruffles, and a powdered wig. The print quality was poor, and the name under the picture was no one I recognised, but there was no mistaking his identity.

It was Morgan Hunt.

Hunt's original name, assuming the portrait was of him and not of his uncannily similar looking ancestor, was Armand de Morganville, and he'd been the only son of a French aristocrat. His father had emigrated to London after the Seven Years' War in the 1760s, when the boy was a couple of years old.

That would make Hunt over two and a half centuries old. Or maybe the father and son were the same person, the "son" taking over when it wasn't plausible for the "father" to look as young anymore. Anything was possible in the chaos of war, especially during an era when records were kept by local churches.

Kane exited his office and spotted me leaning close to the screen. "Busy working?"

"Not really," I confessed, straightening. "I'm doing research."

"For Hunt?" He didn't look pleased by the notion.

"Of Hunt. Look at this." I turned my laptop around, showing him the portrait.

He studied it with narrowed eyes. "Could be his ancestor?"

"If he weren't a vampire, I wouldn't question it for a moment. And even if it is, it's a clue to his origins."

"And what would you do with that information?"

I spread my arms. "Anything. He's the most powerful vampire in town, and he desperately wanted this book, so there has to be a reason for that."

"Maybe he's nostalgic, or embarrassed by the book."

"Or he's hiding something."

He headed to the door with an exasperated shake of his head. "Just don't go inviting trouble. I'll be back around two. I have a client meeting."

Alone again, I read the short chapter of vampires in Bishop's book. It had nothing interesting, and it mostly repeated the myths I'd learned from TV series and fantasy books. Or it was the origin of the myths.

It stated that vampires didn't have a reflection, which I knew to be false, having lived with one for a couple of months; that they could be killed with a wooden stake through the heart—who couldn't?—and that you had to invite them to your home for them to be able to enter, which I hoped was true, but I'd have to ask Luca. There was even the bit about garlic and religious symbols repelling them. I knew Luca loved garlic in his food, but I'd have to ask about the religious symbols.

Either the author of the book had made everything up, or the folklore he claimed to have researched had everything wrong. Or it could be that someone had deliberately given the author misleading information...

Could de Morganville be blamed for it?

Bishop claimed that de Morganville was a real vampire whom he had met in London society. London was growing rapidly at the time of the book's publication, but the high society in which Bishop had belonged to—he was a son of a viscount—was relatively small. It was entirely plausible he'd known Armand de Morganville personally.

The reason he believed Armand to be a vampire was because in the twenty years that the two had frequented the same parties and other high society events in the late eighteen century, de Morganville hadn't aged a day. Age hadn't treated Bishop as kindly; he'd had to retire to his country estate at forty, so he didn't have first-hand knowledge of de Morganville after that. But he claimed Armand had still been the centre of the society, as young and beautiful as ever.

Abandoning the book, I logged on to a genealogy site and searched for Armand de Morganville. Not everything in the archives was digitalised yet, but aristocratic families were more likely to be, even the French émigré ones. I got an instant hit.

According to the records, Armand died in 1806 at forty-five, so he'd been born in 1761. As an unmarried man, he'd left his fortune to Claude, his son from a French opera singer. Claude had adopted his father's name de Morganville.

At that point I had to move to the shop with my laptop so that Mrs Walsh could go have her lunch, but my research came to a halt when Hunt's promised TV arrived. It was brought in by two men who deftly mounted it onto the stand. It worked too. I made them check.

That was one less worry about the auction off my list.

However, there was about a million other tasks left, and I couldn't immediately return to my research. It kept itching at the back of my mind. I had to find a portrait of Claude somewhere, to see if he was Armand, but I had a hunch that Armand had avoided having one made after the one that got printed.

Kane returned from his client meeting in the afternoon, smiling brightly as he placed a small art deco statuette on my desk. "This is for the shop. Can you add it to the online catalogue?"

He'd finally agreed that the shop needed its inventory in a digital form. It was easy to make an online catalogue based on it, but we didn't sell online yet. Kane had absolutely refused it—he believed in personal service—but it did give clients a chance to see what was on offer.

It was a delightful bronze and ivory sculpture from the 1930s by Josef Lorenzl, a famous Austrian sculptor, of a flapper woman dancing with abandon. I stared at it suspiciously and kept my hands tightly against my chest.

He grinned. "It's not cursed."

"I'm not taking any chances."

Still smiling, he picked up the statuette and headed to his office. I followed, as the photography equipment was there.

"Maybe we should add curse detection to your studies," he quipped, and my heart skipped a beat.

"Are you my teacher now?"

Regretfully, he shook his head as he placed the statuette on a small table in the corner that acted as our photo studio. "It's best that Amber handles your education. But I'll be paying close attention."

His words made the pit of my stomach flutter. I hoped it was for anticipation, but more likely it was for fear of failure.

Magic and I were not on good terms.

Nine

AFTER I'D PHOTOGRAPHED THE statuette—which I managed not to touch once—I returned to my tasks. But every chance I had, I researched Armand and his reincarnations.

Claude de Morganville—in his twenties at the time of Armand's "death"—went to India and made a fortune there in emeralds. He married a daughter of an English officer there and had one son, but I couldn't find any official records of either the marriage or the birth. There was only the word of the "son," Robert de Morganville, when he, at twenty, came to England in 1852 after his parents died.

I lost track of him there. If Robert had faked his death and assumed a new name, he would have made sure the fortune was transferred to his new identity, so I'd have to find his will. If he "died" in his forties like the other incarnations, that should be around 1872.

I was busy trying to find portraits of him online when Kane exited his office. "May I offer you a ride home?"

I hadn't even noticed the time; the research had immersed me completely. Grateful for the offer, I gathered my things and followed him to his car.

There was no parking to be had around Oxford Street, so Kane had a reserved spot in a carpark a couple of blocks away. I waited until we were out of the garage and on our way.

"I take it it's not Giselle's cooking that's drawing you to our place a third night in a row?"

His lips tugged to a brief smile, but he shook his head. "I don't like Hunt's summons. I'm coming with Luca and you."

Hunt's high-handed order annoyed me as well, and we would be safer with Kane there, but I hesitated. "What if it angers him?"

"It might," he said, unhelpfully. "But I'll develop an ulcer if I spend the evening worrying about you in his house."

He spared a brief glance at me from traffic. There was both worry and warmth on his face, and my heart skipped an unruly beat.

"In that case, thank you for your sacrifice."

He laughed. "I didn't have anything to sacrifice for this."

Kane found parking by the street outside the House of Magic, and we went in through the shop. Amber was arranging a bookshelf, but she abandoned the task when we entered, and shot a worried look at us.

"Is something amiss?"

Kane's smile was wry. "Do I only visit when it is?" Then he reconsidered. "Although, this is more of a necessary visit."

"Well, Giselle is always happy to have more mouths to feed…"

Third Spell's the Charm

Luca was in the kitchen, dressed up and ready for the evening—or day in his case. I'd given him a heads-up of what we had to do, and he was pleased to see Kane.

"I just hope we won't end up needing you."

That made two of us.

I'd imagined Hunt would live in a rambling manor with turrets and gargoyles, preferably near a misty moor, no matter that those were hard to come by in modern day London. I was therefore utterly disappointed when he turned out to live in one of the modern high-rises by Hyde Park. Architectural wonders to some, eyesores for others. But perhaps new seems more interesting when one has been alive for two and half centuries.

The building had valet parking, so Kane drove his Jag straight to the main entrance and we scrambled out. Or I did, as I was sitting in the back seat, which was not easy to exit from. He gave the keys to the waiting valet and only barely refrained from giving the young man instructions on how the car should be handled.

The lobby was a sleek steel and glass cube, with desks for a concierge and security at one side. The chap manning the first gave us a wide smile, which dimmed a little when he realised we weren't residents.

The security guard was professional and armed; highly illegal, but since the building was owned by Saudi oil sheiks, the family members of whom lived there, probably necessary.

He demanded to know who we were there to see, checked his log, and glared accusingly when Kane's name wasn't on it. He didn't ban Kane outright but called Hunt's flat for confirmation.

"Mr Hunt would be delighted to see you," the security guard said, sounding anything but. He made us sign the log, and then proceeded to pat us down for weapons. I'd been subjected to such procedures at airports occasionally, but never at a private residence. I began to see why Hunt wanted to live here.

"Take the lift on the left. It'll take you to the correct floor, and only there, so don't try to push any buttons."

I was already intimidated, and I hadn't even seen Hunt yet, but Kane merely nodded. "Thank you."

As if it had been waiting, or directed to arrive by security, the doors of the correct lift opened as we crossed the lobby. We filed into the cage and rode the twelve floors up in silence. The back wall was glass, and we had a good view over the atrium in the middle of the building with its large fountains and full-sized trees. It was empty, but I couldn't tell if it was because of the time of the evening or because the beautiful space was completely wasted on the residents.

The lift let us out into a small foyer with a marble floor. There were two doors, and the one on the left was ajar.

"I guess that's our destination," Luca said. He gave the door a perfunctory rap and pushed it open. We filed in, and I only barely stifled a nervous twitch when the door closed behind us.

There was more marble in the entrance hall and nothing much else, only a gilded mirror on the wall—vampires definitely saw their reflections—and a gilded chair with red velvet upholstering that looked like a genuine piece from the eighteenth century. There wasn't even a coat rack, but there was a door that almost disappeared in the marble wall that probably hid a closet.

Hunt wasn't there to greet us, so we walked down the short hallway. It ended at a large room that cut sideways

Third Spell's the Charm

through the building, with windows onto Hyde Park at one end and onto the atrium at the other. The amount of light reaching in had to be staggering on a summer day. Either Hunt didn't have to care anymore, or he had means for blocking it. Both, I'd wager.

The floor was on different levels, creating two platforms at both ends and a deeper space in the middle where lush sofas and divans were set around a large, round gas fireplace that was open to all directions, like a plate with a dome shaped cover hovering over it. The fire was lit. Hunt was standing by it, waiting for us, so we descended the couple of marble steps to him.

He glared at Kane. "I didn't invite you."

Kane shrugged a shoulder minutely. "You didn't specifically forbid me from coming."

"Did you bring my goods?"

I lifted the paper bag containing the items he'd purchased. The security guard hadn't paid any attention to it, which I hadn't registered at the time. I wondered if Kane had hidden it from him somehow.

Of course he had.

I didn't want to go near Hunt, so I placed the bag on one of the settees and retreated hastily. Hunt sneered, but didn't say anything. He didn't pick the bag up either and instead gestured for us to sit.

I dropped hastily onto the nearest seat with Luca. Kane didn't show similar fear, but he sat closer to me than was his habit. I was flanked by two men who knew enough magic to have saved me from a hellhound and a maniac mage, but I still didn't feel entirely safe.

Hunt looked calm and reasonable as he took a seat, so he probably wasn't going to attack. "I went to meet Adam Finch. He is not the vampire I'm looking for."

"How do you know?" The words were out of my mouth before I could consider the wisdom of speaking.

"Let's say he was not … a match for me."

"Is he still alive?" Luca asked, and I tensed. Hunt shrugged.

"He'll live."

Luca probably sensed my worry, because he placed a consoling hand on my forearm. "It's difficult to kill a vampire."

"What, a wooden stake through the heart won't do it?" I quipped feebly.

Hunt gave me an incredulous look. "Where did you get that notion from?"

"*Buffy the Vampire Slayer*?" He only blinked. "You've never watched *Buffy*?"

Admittedly, I'd been a baby when the show aired, but I'd watched it later with my girlfriends.

"Why would I watch a show where my kind is killed?"

"Education?" However, if much of the show relied on the myths in Bishop's book, it couldn't be accurate. I had so many questions, but I'd best save them for Luca later.

Hunt looked disgusted. "Finch and I didn't fight. And he was adamant he hadn't told his boyfriend anything about vampires."

"There went that theory…" I sighed.

"What theory?" Luca asked. Since it wasn't a serious notion, I hadn't told him.

"Maybe Finch wasn't the only vampire dating humans, and a vigilante was killing them to keep vampires a secret."

All three men straightened. "Maybe that's exactly it," Kane said. Hunt nodded too.

"I definitely like it better than the notion that this is an attack against me."

"But why would the killer leave the bodies in the open, if the motive was to keep vampires secret?" Luca pointed out the reason I'd discarded the idea in the first place. "And why would they be in your clubs?"

Kane tapped fingers against his mouth, considering. "A distraction? While Morgan's busy figuring out who is targeting him, the vigilante can continue killing without interruptions."

"That would be a good theory, if vampires didn't habitually kill their food," Hunt pointed out. "I wouldn't have paid any attention if the victims weren't in my clubs."

"Maybe we should check the victims' partners anyway," Luca suggested. "Maybe they're not as randomly chosen as we assumed."

I nodded. "Except two of the victims were here as tourists, and one was on a botched date."

"Doesn't mean she didn't have an ex-boyfriend who is a vampire. Miss Peaches had."

"The girl was twenty," I said, appalled, but Luca only shrugged. Since teenage girls might find dating a vampire exciting—I probably would've—I gave in.

"Fine. That leaves Phan Yên Thu and the nurse, Sherry Beck."

"Who was killed in a club near where Adam Finch lives," Luca pointed out.

"Maybe we should start there," Hunt suggested. "Ask the werewolf guards if they'd seen her hanging out with vampires."

"And I'd like to see the CCTV footage from your clubs from the nights the vampire hunted there," Luca said.

Hunt frowned. "I already watched through them, and didn't recognise anyone."

"But did you watch them back-to-back," asked Luca, "looking for a face that would show up in all of them? I have software that can compare faces."

Hunt looked mildly impressed and he nodded. "If the footage still exists, you can have it."

"Tonight?"

"We can go right away."

Hunt rose and we followed suit, rounding the seating groups to the stairs to the foyer. I'd been too intimidated to look around when we arrived, so I did so now, shamelessly.

I was an antiques dealer in the making. I was allowed.

The walls and all available surfaces were full of art. Some of it was invaluable, but most were average, if old, likely items that Hunt had purchased as new. But they would do well in our shop, if he ever chose to sell any of them.

I noticed with interest some statuettes that were clearly Indian in origin and old. Maybe he'd collected them himself when he was living there as Claude de Morganville.

The paintings were mostly landscapes, some of them of exotic locations, and still-lives. There were old photographs too, and one on a sideboard caught my interest. It was a sepia colour portrait of two men in the formal attire of the late eighteenth-century gentlemen. Their mutton chops were huge, and their stares were frozen like in most photographs of the time. I leaned closer.

"Is this you?" I asked Hunt, my curiosity overriding my common sense again. He was barely recognisable with the beard, but it gave me hope there would be pictures of him elsewhere.

His smile was brief and wistful, gone before I could properly register it. "Yes. Taken in New York in 1881. Harry Glen and I went there to make our fortunes in the railroad business."

"And did you?" I might as well ask everything I wanted to know.

He spread his arms to encompass the room. "As you can see."

"Was your friend a powerful vampire too?"

"No." The message of his curt answer was clear: stop asking questions.

I did, but I marked the name for later as I followed the men out. It was a clue for solving the mystery of Morgan Hunt.

WE ALL FILED INTO Kane's Jag, Luca and I in the back seat, making it even more cramped. Hunt and Kane spent the two-mile drive to Waterloo Station talking about various versions of Jaguars and why this one was the best.

I tuned out for most of it.

The club was located under the elevated railroads on the west side of Waterloo Station. It was a straight street south from St Thomas' Hospital, less than five minutes on foot, which might explain why Sherry Beck, the nurse who had been killed there, had chosen the place.

It was well hidden between two car tunnel lanes going in opposite directions. You had to know it was there to find it. There was no parking, or even stopping, outside it, but at the other end of the tunnel was a large garage for commuters, where we left the car.

The club was rather lamely called Underground, but Hunt told us it wasn't just for the location. "It's a small haven of counterculture and harmless fetishes."

I gave him a disbelieving look from the corner of my eye. With his suits and polished looks, he looked the poster boy of corporate culture. "How do you own it, then?"

"I don't look suitably underground to you?" he sneered, then shrugged. "It was the seventies. Everyone was on acid. Didn't do much for a vampire, but I ended up making some odd purchases."

"And you've kept it all these years," Kane noted, as he held the door to the club open for us to enter.

"I've had no reason to sell it."

I remembered the various items in Hunt's home. When you were as old as him, there probably was a need to cling to some things from the past.

The club opened straight from the door with no vestibule to keep the outside world out. It was like stepping into a dungeon, small and dark, with blacklights making our teeth unnaturally white.

There was a fair crowd for a Tuesday night. Today seemed to be a leather fetish or BDSM night—or maybe it looked like this every night. The music was loud enough to block the sound of trains going overhead and nothing I recognised, but to which I kind of wanted to dance anyway.

I didn't have a chance to get a better look when Hunt already led us through a door behind the ticket booth and into a cramped backroom. A man in black jeans and a T-shirt with the club's logo was manning a security desk there, monitoring the outside of the club and the bar area from a computer screen. He nodded at Hunt respectfully.

"Evening, boss. Didn't expect to see you tonight."

"Evening, Dave. Do we still have footage from that night when the nurse died?"

The security guard nodded. "I saved it especially. Had a hunch that you might want it later."

"Thank you. Excellent job. Would it be possible to get a copy for my investigator?" He nodded at Luca, who pulled up straighter, trying to look like a proper PI.

"You have a vamp doing a wolf's job?" the guy sneered.

Luca sneered back: "When a wolf isn't up to the task…"

A low, hostile growl filled the small room, and I was amazed to realise that Luca was making it too. He was one of the most laidback people I knew.

Hunt's power flared, pressing on me as well, until Kane wrapped an arm around me, shielding me with magic.

"Cut it out," Hunt ordered sharply. "I need the copy now."

Suitably subdued, Dave the security man clicked his computer. "It's on a secure cloud. Where do I send the link to?"

Luca gave him his email address and Dave clicked his computer a bit more.

"Can you contact the other clubs, have them send the footage to Luca too?" Hunt asked, and Dave promised to do it.

"Do you remember Sherry Beck who was killed here?" Luca asked Dave, taking out his phone. He opened it to show the photo to Dave, having apparently taken time to digitise the photos Hunt had sent.

Dave studied the photo with his head tilted, his alert expression reminding me of a dog. Or maybe I was projecting, knowing he was a werewolf.

"She was here quite often," Dave said, giving the phone back. "Random nights, arriving around ten. Always alone."

"Alone?" I asked. "What about her boyfriend?"

Dave shrugged. "She was never here with anyone. She came in, had a glass of water, maybe a pill or something, I don't know, and danced for an hour or two."

I found the image heart-breaking: a nurse trying to unwind from her hectic job any way she could, even if it meant going alone.

"Do you have any vampires coming here regularly?" Kane asked.

"Not so regularly that I would've marked any faces. Wolves like this place. Keeps the bloodsuckers away. No offence," he added hastily, glancing at his boss.

"Where was the body found?" I asked. Hunt's report didn't say, and the club didn't look large enough for keeping a body hidden for more than a few minutes.

"Outside. There's a recess in the wide support column between the lanes right outside our front door. Guys use it as a toilet and sometimes homeless people like to sleep there too. We check it every night after closing. She was dumped there like an old rug."

The image made me wince. Her body had been visible, but not instantly noticeable, just like with Miss Peaches.

We thanked Dave and exited the small room to the club proper. The music was still loud, but not so loud that I wouldn't have heard a delighted, "Phoebe! Luca!"

Ten

WE TURNED TO THE VOICE TO see Ashley cross the floor to us from the bar where she'd been queueing, pushing past people blocking her way. She was wearing leather trousers and a V-neck leather vest with the zipper left open at the top to give a glimpse of her cleavage. She had even more piercings than normal, and there was a bronze bracelet around her impressive bicep. She looked sexy, fierce, and scary.

"What are you doing here?" I asked, baffled.

"I came to unwind. It's near our station and many of my kind come here often."

Luca gave her a pointed look. "You said you hate these places."

She tilted her head, showing us black earplugs blocking her ears. "These help a little." She glanced over us and straightened, nodding respectfully. "Archibald. Who's the vamp?"

"Morgan Hunt," Luca introduced him. "He owns the club."

She perked. "Is this one of the places you're investigating?"

"Yes."

"Can I come with you? There's no one interesting here tonight."

"I think we're mostly done for tonight," Luca said, "but your company is always welcome."

Ashley wrapped an arm around his shoulder, steering him towards the door. "Aww, thanks."

They both laughed as they exited. I followed hastily, grateful to escape the heat and stale air of the club. I took a gulp of fresh air the moment I was out of the door—or as fresh as it could be in a tunnel busy with cars even at that time of evening.

My inhale turned to a startled cough when a man stepped from behind the column outside the door, and pointed a weapon at us.

"Morgan Hunt, you killed my girlfriend. Now you must die."

Several things happened simultaneously. I froze, in surprise rather than fear. Kane stepped in front of me, hand thrown towards the shooter, his hair billowing in preparation of a spell. Ashley rushed at the shooter, fangs lengthening in anticipation of a fight to death. Luca and Hunt mesmerised the shooter, the competing commands causing the man to pass out and collapse on the pavement.

It was over in seconds, with no one hurt—unless you count the shooter passing out—without the gun discharging. I fought to capture my breath, the coughing spell not quite over, made worse by a realisation that in a dire situation I was useless.

It wasn't simply that I couldn't cast spells. It didn't even occur to me to try to defend myself, not to mention other people, with or without magic.

Ashley growled, her fangs returning to their normal size. I'd seen her in full wolf-form, but this sort of partial shift was new and looked somehow more frightening. She leaned over the shooter and removed the weapon. She made sure the safety was on and slipped it into the waistband of her trousers at the small of her back like in action movies, her movements so calm and practiced that I knew she had done it before.

"What should I do with him?" she asked Hunt. His lip curled in disgust.

"Bring him inside. I need to talk to him."

Seemingly without effort, she pulled the shooter into a fireman's carry and headed back in. Our re-entry with an unconscious man caused the people in the club to pause and stare at us. I resisted the urge to give them a small wave, but I couldn't stifle a hysterical giggle.

Being held at gunpoint did not bring out the best in me.

Dave stepped out of the security room and held the door open for Ashley, the look in his eyes wary but respectful. Maybe Ashley was more powerful than him. In books, werewolves had all sorts of power structures based on strength, but I didn't know if that applied to real life.

My money would be on Ashley in a fight between them.

We filed into the cramped room. Ashley lowered the shooter onto a chair, but remained right behind him. The man was maybe in his mid-thirties, with short russet hair cropped close to the skull, and the sturdy body of a rugby player, but he wouldn't be a threat. Kane gestured with his fingers and then nodded at Hunt.

"He's immobilised."

I hated that spell, having been subjected to it by bad people before, but it was useful.

Hunt revived the man with magic of his own. His eyes opened, bleary at first and then bewildered. "Where am I?" He tried to sit up. "Why can't I move? Who are you?"

Hunt sneered. "I'm Morgan Hunt." There was no recognition in the man's eyes. "The man you just tried to shoot?"

"What? Why...?" He looked around, trying to move again. "I don't even own a gun."

Ashley pulled it out and showed it to him. "Where did this come from, then?"

The man only stared at it, uncomprehending.

"What's your name?" I asked, more gently than Hunt's interrogation.

"Ummm ... Peter? Robinson?"

"You're not sure?"

He shook his head. "I ... it's a bit fuzzy." He frowned, puzzled.

I glanced at Hunt. "Could your ... thing have messed with his mind?" I wiggled my fingers, not wanting to say the word mesmerising aloud, but he understood.

"It shouldn't have this kind of effect."

"What is the last thing you remember?" Kane asked. Peter squinted his eyes, struggling to remember.

"I ... was coming home from work. I've been working late since my girlfriend..." He swallowed "...died. I was holding my keys, about to open the door." He paused, shaking his head. "I can't remember anything between that moment and here."

Hunt gestured with his hand and Peter's eyes glazed over. "Someone's messed with his mind, given him a command to come here and shoot me."

Third Spell's the Charm

"Two guesses who it was," Luca said with a grim nod.

"But how would he have found Peter?" I asked, baffled. "The victims are random. I doubt he knew their names, let alone anything about their families."

Kane nodded, agreeing. "And how did the vampire know to send Peter here, so fast?"

The last question made Hunt growl. "The fucker's keeping tabs on me."

We all glanced around, as if the vampire were here, watching us.

"I don't think anyone was following us," Kane said, frowning. "But I wasn't looking for a tail."

"He didn't have to, if he can make humans obey his commands this well," Luca said. "He could've programmed someone in the club staff to call him the moment you showed up. Maybe your building security too, if he knew to go to Peter this fast."

"Fuck."

Hunt's power began to rise again, pressing against me, making it difficult to breathe. Ashley and Dave began to growl quietly, and the pressure cut.

"Is there anything we can learn from this man's mind?" Kane asked. "Who it was that gave him the command, maybe?"

Hunt looked aggravated. "No, we're not mind readers. Do mages have anything?"

Kane shook his head. "Hypnosis might work, but I don't know anyone who's skilled with it."

"I might as well wipe his mind again and give him a new memory," Hunt said, disgusted, his body still taut with anger. "Hopefully it takes after this many scramblings. Can you release him?"

Kane let the magical restraints go and Peter slumped in the chair. Hunt revived him and quickly captured his mind. "You remember nothing of tonight. When you enter your home, it's exactly what you meant to do when you left work, later than usual."

Dave walked Peter out and we followed. A command from Hunt sent Peter on his way. We followed from a distance until he walked past the garage where Kane's car was.

I watched him head to the station. "I really don't understand what the point was of sending Peter to shoot you."

"It's an escalation of the vampire's attack against me," Hunt said.

"But if he can do that, why didn't he send someone to kill you from the start instead of killing the humans?"

"Thanks," Hunt said dryly.

Luca smiled. "Old vampires hold grudges. Simply killing Morgan won't satisfy."

"I believe it's time we try to figure out who from your past hates you this much," I suggested. Hunt paused outside Kane's Jag.

"Just concentrate on the present and leave my past be."

"Why?"

"I've spent a long time hiding my past. You won't find anything useful."

I nodded, but I wouldn't obey. I knew where to look. I didn't need his help to unravel the truth.

Kane opened the door to his Jag and Luca was about to climb into the back seat when Ashley halted him. "We won't all fit," she stated with contempt. "You and Phoebe will ride in my car."

Third Spell's the Charm

"Are you headed home?" Kane asked. Luca and I glanced at each other.

"Is there anything more we can do tonight?" I asked.

"Maybe we should check the family of the Vietnamese girl, in case the vampire sends them after Hunt next," Luca suggested.

"They live in Brighton," Hunt said. "The girl was here without their permission on a date. I doubt the vampire can make them come after me."

"The relatives of that Nigerian tourist live in London, but the German boy didn't have family here," Luca said. "And then there's Adam Finch, but he can't be mesmerised, so the vampire won't use him. And if we couldn't locate the family of Miss Peaches beyond him, I doubt the vampire can."

"How about her friends at the cabaret?" I asked.

Luca pursed his lips. "He might try there. It's the only place her social media leads to. Besides, we should tell Shepard that he can stop looking for her family." He glanced at his wristwatch.

"The evening show will end soon. We might just make it there in time."

"We can't all go," I protested. "We'll frighten them if we descend on them with such a large group."

Hunt nodded. "Very well. You go. Archibald, can you give me a lift home?"

Kane nodded and they got into his Jag with quick goodbyes. I could see Kane wanted to tell me to be careful, but it was a cabaret and I was with a vampire and a werewolf. I would be safe.

Luca and I climbed into Ashley's large Land Rover. "Where to?" she asked. I told her and she got a dreamy look in her eyes.

"I love their food. Do you think the kitchen is still open?"

THE KITCHEN HAD CLOSED for the night already, much to Ashley's disappointment. Only the bar was open. There weren't many people around, but judging by the alert looks of the staff, they expected the people exiting the cabaret to stay for a glass or two.

We went straight downstairs, where cheerful music came through the closed doors of the theatre. It sounded like fun. I realised with a pang in my chest that if things had gone differently, we would've been in the audience tonight as Miss Peaches's guests. I would've loved to see her perform.

The same usher as before was leaning against the low counter of the cloak room, chatting with the woman minding the coats, waiting for the show to end. He straightened when he spotted us.

"Are you here to see Maxim? You might still catch him if you're quick." Luca nodded and the usher spoke to his microphone. The conversation was brief. "He's coming down."

Maxim Shepard exited the door from backstage just as loud applause in the theatre signalled that the show had ended. He was wearing the same red leather jacket, but had paired it with the kind of billowing shirt that men were using before the invention of industrial buttonholes, like Colin Firth in *Pride and Prejudice* and glam rockers of the eighties. He could pull off the look.

He smiled at us, then tilted his head and studied Ashley with an appreciative gleam in his eyes. There was a lot to look at; she hadn't even worn a coat over her bare arms.

Third Spell's the Charm

"I could put you on stage and make you a star."

Ashley's nostrils flared. The man reeked of cologne and cigar smoke; even I could smell it. "I think I prefer fighting fires to performing for audiences, thanks."

"Pity." He turned his attention to Luca. "Did you find Sam's family?"

Luca nodded. "We found the ex-boyfriend and told him what had happened. If the family can be found, he'll inform them."

Shepard looked grim. "Good. I wouldn't have been able to hold the news much longer. I'd best tell the performers right away."

The usher opened the doors to the theatre and the first people began to file out while the applause was still going on. Shepard gestured at the backstage door.

"Let's wait here for the stage to clear."

There was a great hustle and bustle in the hallway behind the stage as the performers retreated there and then headed back on the stage for one more round of thankyous. There were more feathers, plumes, boas, and sequins than I'd ever seen in one place, worn by people who thought nothing of hurrying around in five-inch heels.

Soon the stage quieted as the audience left and the usher closed the doors to the theatre. Maxime Shepard clapped his hands together and raised his voice to be heard over the noise the dozens of performers made.

"Everyone back on the stage. I have an announcement to make."

It took quite a bit of herding before everyone was on the stage, some grumbling about the delay to leaving for home, but most of them curious.

"You'd best announce that Miss Peaches will be back for tomorrow's show, because that bitch almost ruined my main number," the queen with the biggest plume announced, pointing at someone at the side of the group.

"Fuck you, bitch. If you hadn't deliberately stepped in front of me, I would've handled it perfectly."

Shepard clapped his hands again. "Shut up. This is important." He inhaled, gathering himself as the people quieted. "I'm sorry to have to tell you this, but Sam—Miss Peaches—is dead."

Stunned silence fell. Then everyone spoke at once, some asking questions, others denying his news, and some bursting into tears. Miss Peaches's understudy looked genuinely distraught; the main diva less so, despite having hoped for her return.

A question finally got through: "How did she die and when?"

Maxim Shepard turned to us. "You have the details."

We hadn't agreed on a story, but this wasn't the first time Luca had had to invent something for the loved ones of a vampire's victim, even if his killing days were almost a century behind him.

"There was an accident as she was leaving a club on Saturday night. She hit her head and couldn't be revived. She died later in the hospital."

"Why are we hearing about this only now?" the main diva demanded.

"I'm sorry, we needed to locate the next of kin first. We're having some trouble finding them though. Would any of you know about her family?"

Everyone shook their heads. "I think she'd cut ties completely."

"Has anyone else been asking after her family recently?" I asked.

"Like that ex-boyfriend of hers?"

"We already informed him. He seemed to believe people here would know more." I didn't look specifically at Shepard, but I'd got a notion that Adam Finch believed Shepard should've known.

Everyone shook their heads. It had been a long shot anyway. Even if the vampire had asked about her family, he would've wiped their memories.

I glanced at Luca, but he shrugged, indicating he had nothing to ask, so I thanked everyone. "I'm sorry for your loss," I added, before leaving them to hug and console each other.

We returned to the lobby and crossed it to the stairs up. Ashley shook herself like a dog. "Uh. I'm glad we didn't stay longer."

"Why? Too many feathers to your liking?" I teased, and she rolled her eyes, though her mouth quirked. The contrast with the cheerful outfits of the performers and her black leathers had been amusing.

"No, it reeked of vampire there."

Eleven

WE PAUSED SO ABRUPTLY SHE WAS several steps up the stairs before she noticed and turned to look. "What?"

"It didn't occur you to tell us?" Luca demanded. "We're looking for a vampire."

She shrugged, and continued up. We rushed after her. "I didn't sense a vampire there. There was just a smell."

"What does that mean?" I asked. There were people at the top of the stairs, so she couldn't answer until we were out of the door and on our way to her car.

"It means that a vampire has been hanging out there, recently."

"Could you tell who?" Luca asked.

"You mean you couldn't smell it yourself?"

"I don't detect vampires by their scent, just their power. And there wasn't a vampire present. Besides, Shepard reeked so strongly I couldn't smell anything else."

She sneered, affectionately. "Weaknose."

"Just tell me." We paused outside her car, and she shrugged.

"I don't know who it was. Everything smelled of a vampire. Even through all the horrid perfumes."

"Just one?"

She pulled the car key out of her pocket and triggered the remote locks. "Yes. And it was a stronger scent than what you give out."

"Does that mean it's a stronger vampire too?" I asked as I climbed on the backseat. "Or that he's spent a longer time there?"

"We've been looking for a strong vampire," Luca said. "I couldn't sense a vampire there, but we already know that doesn't mean a vampire wasn't present."

"Or they'd left right before we came," Ashley mused.

"Basically, then, the vampire could've contacted people at the cabaret already, messed with their minds to send them after Hunt, and we'd be none the wiser?" I summarised, and Luca dipped his chin.

"Yep."

I threw my hands up. "Then how the hell are we going to find this vampire?"

For all we knew, one of the performers could've been him, standing right under our noses, pretending to mourn Miss Peaches while chuckling to themself for our ignorance. Everyone wore such heavy makeup it was impossible to tell what they looked like underneath.

Luca looked confident. "I have the CCTV footage. I'll set my facial recognition software to work on it. Hopefully we'll be much wiser come the morning."

But when the morning came, it was with a new twist.

"Have you seen this headline?"

I was having breakfast when Luca walked into the kitchen and dropped a newspaper in front of me. An actual, physical newspaper, not an online article.

Third Spell's the Charm

"I went for a morning jog and spotted it at a news stand."

"So you do exercise," I teased, but he just pointed at the paper.

It was the front page, and the story took main half of it, though mostly because the font was so large: *Gun attack at a nightclub!*

The story described amazingly accurately what had happened last night, naming Hunt not only as the target of the attack but the owner of the club too.

"Bugger," I said with feeling. "While we were chasing people connected with Miss Peaches, the vampire contacted the press."

"Yeah..." Luca sat heavily at the table. "What are the chances Hunt won't notice this?"

A low growl sounded behind us. "Non-existent."

I tensed, not wanting to face Hunt. It was too early in the morning for irate vampires.

Luca was braver. "Morgan. What an unexpected ... pleasure." The amendment came after I kicked him under the table.

"I gave you one job," Hunt began, but was interrupted by Giselle, who was beaming at him as if he wasn't in a foul mood.

"Good morning. Mr Hunt, is it? Would you like some tea?"

He looked bemused, but centuries of good manners won. "I'd love some."

"And make it as calming as possible," I muttered, but the vampire had excellent hearing.

"That won't save you from my ire."

"What do you want us to say?" Luca demanded. "That we anticipated this and did nothing? And even if we had, there are so many different forms of media he could've used that we couldn't possibly have stopped him."

Hunt glowered at him, but took a seat when Giselle set a beautiful teacup for him she only reserved for important guests. "Would you like some breakfast too? We have plenty, though Ashley had all the bacon already before she left to work."

You could tell the approaching full moon by the amount of meat she consumed.

"No, thank you. Tea will be fine."

Giselle poured the tea for him, the scent revealing it was her calming evening tea. I shot her an amused look, and she dimpled at me. Hunt recognised the scent too.

"This won't have any effect on me."

"Doesn't hurt to try," Giselle said, unperturbed.

He picked up the cup, his hold elegant. Even centuries couldn't wipe away some habits. I could instantly picture the eighteenth-century aristocrat in his portrait.

He took a sip and gave an approving nod at Giselle. "Excellent tea, madam."

Giselle beamed at him, but if I'd hoped his mood would improve, I was wrong.

"Now, what do you intend to do about this mess?"

I knew exactly what I was going to do: nothing. But I couldn't say that aloud. Luca was braver.

"My facial recognition software is still running. There's a ton of material for it to go through, from the moment the doors opened to when they closed that night, from five clubs. I don't expect results anytime soon."

That did not please Hunt. "Why did I hire you if you can't produce results?"

Luca straightened, incensed. "You didn't hire me, you extorted me. And how am I to narrow down the suspects

Third Spell's the Charm

when you probably have enemies that stretch back centuries."

"If it was someone from my past, they would've acted before now," Hunt stated.

I disagreed. "You people change identities so often your enemies have lost track of you. Maybe this one's only now found you and needs to press on before you disappear again."

"And if it's a present enemy, it would be helpful to have a name. Or a list of them," Luca added dryly.

"Besides, you'd know if you'd made an enemy of a powerful vampire within the last couple of years."

The sounds of a person running up the stairs made us pause and face the hallway to see who it could be. Ashley was the only one of us with that much energy and she was at work.

To my profound amazement and not so little shock, Kane burst into the kitchen wearing running leggings and a windbreaker, the zipper of which he'd opened, revealing a form-hugging technical T-shirt that emphasised his torso in detail that made my mouth go dry. His hair was mussed and he was slightly flushed, but in a healthy way, not like he was about to have a heart attack in our kitchen.

He paused when he saw our company. "Ah, Morgan. I guess you've heard the news, then?"

"Evidently."

"I noticed the headlines when I ran past a newsagent and decided to drop by on my morning jog to give you a heads-up."

"You ran all the way from Belgravia to here?" Giselle exclaimed, amazed and impressed. I was both too, but I'd swallowed my tongue and couldn't speak. "That's almost four miles! Would you like tea or something else to drink?"

Kane gave her a warm smile. "A glass of water would be wonderful before I need to head back."

She hurried to fill a glass for him. He turned back to Hunt. "Will you be able to weather this?"

Hunt brushed the concern aside. "Of course. I employ professional PR people who will handle it. But it is a next stage in the attack against me, and I don't like that he's taken it public."

"Where will it go from here?" Luca asked. "There hasn't been any clear pattern in his actions. He opened with deaths, and now this."

Hunt shrugged. "If he's from an era when a gentleman's reputation mattered, he might think this is worse."

The old photo of him and his friend, Henry Glenn, rose to my mind. Hunt had said that Glenn hadn't been a vampire, but a gentleman's word had been sacred during the Victorian era. Maybe Hunt had violated that, and now Glenn's progeny wanted revenge. I'd best return to my research into Hunt's past, no matter what he said.

Giselle gave Kane the glass and he drank deeply, making his throat work. I'd never noticed his throat before. It was always covered with the collar of his shirt and a tie. My mouth went so dry my tongue stuck to the roof of my mouth.

These glimpses of Archibald Kane as not a properly behaving gentleman in suits tended to wreak havoc with my emotions.

A sharp kick in my ankle made me jump and glare at Luca, whose eyes were brimming with laughter. "Your boss asked you a question."

Third Spell's the Charm

"Huh?"

Kane's lips quirked, but if he'd noticed how mesmerised I'd been with is drinking, he mercifully didn't say anything. "I'll be away for most of the day. Can you hold the fort?"

"Yes ... of course." I often did. "Most of the preparations for Saturday are done anyway."

"Excellent. If you like, you can take the morning off."

"I ... National Gallery?" I managed to say.

"The Vermeer exhibition? Excellent idea. I'll see you in the afternoon, then."

With that, he headed down the hall and disappeared into the stairs. Luca guffawed. "Man, that was embarrassing."

"I don't know what you're talking about," I said primly, heat rising to my cheeks.

"Right..."

Giselle patted my shoulder. "I was taken with his appearance too, and I prefer women."

I shot a vindicated look at Luca, who wouldn't stop laughing. I punched his shoulder lightly. "If you don't stop that, I'll make you come with me to see the Vermeer exhibition."

He wiped his eyes. "You know what, I actually might come with you."

"You need to work on identifying the killer," Hunt said, but his eyes were amused too when he looked at me. I hadn't drooled that obviously, had I?

"I doubt the software will give any results until tomorrow," Luca answered Hunt.

"Well, keep me posted."

Hunt rose from the table, and with a nod to Giselle, left.

I slumped over the table. "I do not need this much excitement this early in the morning."

"One might even say arousing..." Luca teased. I punched him in the shoulder again, and then pushed myself up.

"I'd best head to work. Shall we meet at the museum?"

"Are you really going to see the Vermeer exhibition?"

"Yes. But I want to visit the portrait gallery too."

His brows shot up. "Why?"

"Because I need to track all Hunt's previous identities. Since I don't know the names, I'll have to go by his face."

"Tracking a vampire's past is frowned upon among my kind."

I winked. "Good thing I'm not your kind, then."

THE NATIONAL GALLERY didn't open until ten, so I headed to work as normal. There were always last-minute preparations when one was organising an auction.

But after I'd handled the morning mail and some online enquiries, I had free time to continue my research into Hunt's past. I clicked onto the National Portrait Gallery's website and the online catalogue for nineteenth century photographs there, and searched for Robert de Morganville, the alleged grandson of Armand de Morganville, aka Morgan Hunt.

To my disappointment, I found nothing, and the system didn't enable a search by an existing photo. I scratched my chin, trying to come up with other options, and remembered Henry Glenn, the man from the photo at Hunt's home.

I had an instant hit. Three photos, one of which was the same I'd seen earlier at Hunt's. And the photo ID named the companion, aka Hunt: Herman Robson. It was

Third Spell's the Charm

a good solid name, but Hunt hadn't been able to resist using his previous names. Herman was the anglicised form or Armand, and Robson was a nod at his previous identity as Robert the Morganville.

Gotcha!

I made an online search of the two names together, which produced a couple of American newspaper articles. They contained nothing interesting, and definitely nothing that would indicate that Henry Glenn would be the enemy from Hunt's past.

I made another search for Herman Robson and learned that Hunt hadn't lied when he said he'd made his fortune in the States—or another fortune, since he'd already made one in emeralds. Maybe Glenn hadn't been as lucky and was holding a grudge? Just because he hadn't been a vampire when Hunt knew him didn't mean he hadn't become one later.

One of the newspaper articles had a photo of Herman Robson, without the mutton chops this time. There was no question about it: it was Morgan Hunt. It was an obituary from 1884, and the cause of death was an explosion at a railroad construction site that had obliterated his entire body.

An effective way to fake one's death.

It didn't list any next of kin, so I had no additional names to search. I saved the photo to my phone, in case I could use it at the National Portrait Gallery. Now I only had to track him through various identities until I found the past enemy who would come after him with such force in present.

Easy…

Luca came to fetch me, and we took the Tube to Charing Cross, neither of us feeling like walking. There would be enough of that in the museum.

We reached the National Gallery right as it opened, only to discover we weren't the only people who wanted to see the exhibition in its last days. The queue reached from the entrance at the Sainsbury Wing to the nearest column on Trafalgar Square. We eyed it in dismay.

"How badly do you want to see it?" Luca asked. I sighed.

"I'd sort of set my heart on it. I love Vermeer's paintings. But I can come back later. Let's head to the Portrait Gallery."

"What do you think you can find there that you can't with an online search?"

I headed towards Charing Cross Road to round the National Gallery to the Portrait Gallery behind it. "Not everything is digitised. I thought I'd wander aimlessly around the museum and hope that a familiar face surfaces on the walls."

"Hunt's?"

"Or the killer's. They had to be there yesterday to witness the shooting. How else could they describe the events so well? Maybe we've seen him and don't even know. Twice now, if you count the club on Saturday too."

He shrugged. "I've got nothing better to do."

We chose a more sensible approach, though, than just wandering around the museum. I asked to see the curator of the late Victorian photos and we were directed to the office of Dr Jane McAllister, a small woman in her late fifties who had embraced the stereotypical look of a librarian with her pleated skirt and cardigan, her greying hair in a bun.

Third Spell's the Charm

I introduced us and asked if it was possible to browse the photo collection without specific keywords or names. Her brows shot up.

"That's quite a lot of photos to go through. Just because the technology was new during the Victorian era doesn't mean there aren't thousands of photos in our gallery from that time."

"If we have a reference photo, is there any way to do a comp search?" Luca asked.

"Yes, though our programme isn't terribly accurate if you only use one photo. And not everything is digitised, of course."

"It's a start," I said.

She led us to a space for academic researchers and logged us onto a computer there. "This isn't online, so you have to upload any photos you want to compare through the USB port. And you can't download anything without permission."

With her help, I uploaded the photo of Herman Robson I'd saved on my phone and then added the photo of him and Glenn that was already in their collection, and she left us to it.

It was slow work. The programme produced results from time to time, all of them of wrong people, and we had to discard them before it would continue. I had time to answer some work emails, and Luca played online poker.

The computer pinged again, and I gave the screen a distracted glance, only to look again. I leaned closer. "This is definitely Hunt!"

It was a newer photo than those I was using as a comparison. The date was 1898, and the place was Waterloo Station, the opening of Waterloo & City Tube line. Hunt was posing with two other men, all in elegant suits and full beards; Hunt's was neatly trimmed. They were standing in front of a satin ribbon that would be ceremoniously cut to declare the line open.

One of the men was listed as Robert Gascoyne-Cecil, the prime minister at the time. I didn't remember the name, but I guessed he had to be the one in the middle, because the third man definitely wasn't him.

My mouth dropped open.

Twelve

"THAT'S ADAM FINCH," I managed to say.

Luca put away his phone and took a look. He read the name on the photo ID. "George Vaughn. He was using that name when I first met him. I didn't know he was older than me." He looked miffed by the realisation.

"He hasn't gone far from Waterloo Station in over a century," I said dryly, and he tilted his head.

"He said he'd only lived there for a decade. I guess that was just in his current identity."

"Which one do you think he is, the chief engineer or the owner of the Waterloo & City Tube line?"

He rolled his eyes. "Definitely the engineer. Hunt has always been the money man."

"If Finch is Vaughn, that makes Hunt Emerson Claude." It was my turn to roll eyes. "He really has no imagination with his names."

"How would you know?"

I realised that in all this I hadn't shared with him the research I'd done. I did so now, much to his amazement. When I was done, I listed the names, holding my fingers for each.

"From Armand de Morganville to Claude and Robert de Morganville, then Herman Robson, which has a clear link to the previous name, and then Emerson Claude. Emerson sounds like Herman's son and Claude refers to that earlier name."

He nodded, impressed. "You've really put your mind to this. What is it for?"

"It started as idle curiosity. But now I'm convinced that somewhere in his past there is the vampire we're looking for, no matter what he claims."

"Do you think it's Finch?"

I spread my arms. "I don't know. Here we have undisputable evidence that the two of them knew each other already in the nineteenth century. But if it's Finch, this would've come to some sort of solution when Hunt spoke to him."

"Hunt said Finch isn't powerful enough to be the vampire we're looking for."

"Maybe Hunt lied. Or perhaps Finch is so powerful he can pretend to be weak?"

His mouth quirked. "That's quite a conjecture."

"Whoever it is, he has to be old. We need to go backwards in Hunt's life."

Luca scratched his neck. "Just because the vampire is old doesn't meant the feud is."

He was right.

"Then what do you suggest we do? Because we can't just wait for the vampire to make another move."

He sighed. "You're right. The answer to all this is in Hunt's past. And here we have the closest link to it we'll ever get."

"You mean Finch?"

"Yes. Let's go talk to him."

Third Spell's the Charm

It was a twenty-minute walk across the Thames over Jubilee Bridge for pedestrians. It had seemed like we'd been forever in the museum, but it was only a little past midday when we were knocking on Finch's door. There was no answer.

"Do you think he's at work?" Luca asked.

I hadn't even considered the possibility that he wouldn't be at home. But if he was older than Luca, he had to be able to face daylight too.

A realisation hit and I tensed. "He must've been strong enough to go out during the day already a century ago when they opened that Tube line. I doubt they did it at night."

Luca's mouth pursed. "He could've travelled underground there..."

That was possible. "But could he have studied to become an engineer at night? Let alone become a chief engineer of an underground construction? That took skill."

"Maybe he studied by correspondence?"

But he didn't sound like he believed it. I gave him a pointed look. "Finch could be as old as Hunt. Or older."

"Then why would Hunt claim otherwise?"

I spread my arms. "I don't know. Maybe we should ask him."

His eyes grew large. "You ask him. I'm staying as far away from him as I can."

"It's a bit too late to keep your distance now," I said dryly.

Finch's door opened all of a sudden. Startled, we twirled around and came face to face with the last person I expected—or wanted—to see.

Danielle Mercer. Kane's ex-wife.

DANIELLE WAS STUNNED to see us, as if we hadn't been knocking on the door only moments ago. She pulled the door hastily closed behind her, not giving us even a glimpse inside to see if Finch was there.

She crossed her arms over her chest. "What are you doing here?"

She was in her late thirties, my height, but so dainty she appeared smaller, with a sharp chin, slightly downturned green eyes, full lips with some lines around them, and short dark brown hair that fell asymmetrically past her left eye. She was more striking than beautiful, but you wouldn't easily forget her.

Kane hadn't.

She was a mage who had embraced the dark side of magic, the reason she and Kane had divorced. She'd been absent from his life for over a decade, only to surface a couple of months ago to try and kill him.

Well, she'd tried to curse him, but I'd triggered the curse instead. Needless to say, it hadn't endeared her to me.

In the aftermath of breaking the curse, she'd disappeared to France with her boyfriend, Laurent Dufort—if you could call a century old warlock *boy*friend—and there she was supposed to stay. So I was perfectly entitled to ask:

"Me? What are you doing here? Shouldn't you be with your hunk of a warlock in France, sacrificing sheep for dark powers?"

She rolled her eyes. "I have business here."

"With Finch?" Luca demanded, and she shot him a contemptuous glance.

Third Spell's the Charm

"He needed the services of a mage, and most of my kind are too good to deal with vampires." Meaning everyone not practicing the dark arts.

"And you're helping him for the goodness of your heart?" I asked.

"Hardly," she sneered. "He's paying me handsomely."

"And what are you doing for him?"

She pursed her lips, but then shrugged. "Wards, if you must know."

That was interesting. "What does he need them for? Is someone after him?"

"What's that to you?"

It would be easier to get information out of her if she weren't such a bitch. "There's a powerful vampire in town causing trouble. If it's not Adam Finch, he knows who it is. Is he home? We need to talk to him."

"What about?"

It was my turn to roll eyes. "His past as the chief engineer of Waterloo & City line. What do you think?"

She glanced behind her at the closed door. "He's not home."

"Yet you're here?"

"It's easier to ward an empty house."

I guess that made sense. It was disappointing though. I turned to Luca. "We have to go talk with Hunt, then."

She sneered. "Good luck with that." She didn't say more but crossed the narrow street to her white Fiat 500. If I'd paid any attention, I would've spotted it and realized she was here.

Then again, London was full of those cars.

"Are you planning to stay in town?" I shouted after her. She shot me a look over her shoulder.

"What do you care?"

"I don't, but the leader of the mages' council might want to know if there's a dark mage hanging around."

She sneered. "I'll inform Archie myself if I need."

She called Kane Archie, which was probably why he preferred to be called Kane these days.

"He isn't the council leader anymore."

She paused and turned to face us. "He's not? What happened?"

"Rupert decided that his skills are put in better use by learning how to become the next archmage."

Her eyes flashed in fury, and she dove into her car, throwing the door closed with greater force than necessary. I wrapped an arm around Luca's and dragged him down the street towards Waterloo Station. He waited until we were out of sight before grinning.

"That wasn't nice."

The reason Danielle had gone to the warlock in the first place was because Rupert had refused to make her his apprentice.

"I don't like that she's back in town. And I especially don't like that she's hanging around Finch."

"It seems like a huge coincidence," he nodded.

"Should we tell Kane?"

He grimaced. "I guess we have to. We need him anyway."

"What for?"

"If you think I'm meeting with Hunt without Kane as a buffer, you're mental."

He had a point.

"Maybe we should postpone going to Hunt and return here later tonight," I suggested. I wasn't eager to involve

Third Spell's the Charm

Hunt either. Besides, he'd all but forbidden us to search his past. "Finch's bound to be home then."

He nodded. "What do you want to do in the meanwhile?"

"I need to head back to work before Kane returns. But I need lunch first."

Luca wanted lunch too, so we headed into Waterloo Station, made our way down the steep escalators, and navigated the underground tunnels to Bakerloo line.

"I find it incredible that Hunt would've had his hands in building this," I said to Luca when I spotted the signs to Waterloo & City line. Despite my fear of Hunt, I couldn't help admiring him a little too.

"I know. I haven't even considered building anything lasting in my time here."

"You're still young," I teased. "Maybe he didn't start building until he was over a hundred himself."

"I'd need a complete personality transplant for that to happen." Laughing, we headed to the platform.

WE EXITED THE TUBE at Piccadilly Circus and headed towards Brasserie Noël. We'd been there twice already without eating, and I was determined to correct that. And it gave Luca a chance to try to sense vampires there. Not that I was hopeful that the killer would return—or that Luca would sense him even if he did.

But I was wrong. We'd finished the excellent meal and were waiting to pay, when Luca tensed. "A vampire's approaching."

I studied the room. "From downstairs?"

"No, outside."

I turned to look out of the window just as Adam Finch reached for the restaurant door.

143

"What's he doing here?" I hissed, though I don't know why I lowered my voice. It wasn't like he could hear us. Besides, we wanted to meet him.

"Maybe he's here to fetch Miss Peaches's belongings?" Luca suggested when Finch headed down the stairs to the theatre.

"Or maybe he's the killer and he's here to mess with the performers' heads to send them after Hunt."

The waiter arrived just then, and Luca couldn't answer. He paid hastily for both of us, and I decided not to argue about it. We needed to move, and I could pay for him later.

The moment the waiter left we gathered our belongings and went after Finch. The downstairs lobby was quiet and empty, but the door to the theatre was open. We peeked in and saw a cleaner mopping the stage floor.

"Finch must've gone through here," Luca said, slipping into the theatre. It was a small room with seating groups around small tables at the front and a couple of rising rows of seats behind them. Walls and upholstering were deep red with accents of faded gold.

The cleaner didn't pay us any attention as we climbed on the stage and headed to the backstage.

"Finch must've mesmerised him," Luca noted grimly.

"Would he have done that if he were here on a legitimate business?"

"Let's find out."

The hallway behind the stage was quiet and the dressing rooms were dark. If Finch had come here, he hadn't stayed.

"Maybe he's upstairs talking with Shepard," I suggested.

"Why would he talk with him?"

"You said it yourself, maybe he's here to fetch Miss Peaches's belongings."

"For which he needed to mesmerise the cleaner?" he said in a dubious voice, but he was already heading up the stairs.

Hurrying up two flights of stairs after a heavy meal left me breathless, but Luca was already entering Shepard's office, so I couldn't pause to catch it.

He stopped so abruptly on the threshold that I collided with him.

The room was empty. "What is it?"

"There's been a been a struggle here."

To my eyes, the mess was as bad as the previous time. "How can you tell?"

"Magic has been used, mage magic, not ours, and Shepard's chair is overturned."

I couldn't sense anything. "Finch can't do mage magic. And why would he attack Shepard?"

"Maybe Shepard is a mage?"

I hadn't come to think of it. "Then why would he attack Finch?"

He looked around, as if the men would miraculously materialise. His nostrils flared. "I don't know, but I have a bad feeling about this…"

He hurried to the stairs to the restaurant and was halfway down before I'd reached the first step, only to return equally fast, forcing me to turn around. "They're not in the restaurant."

"They didn't go through the theatre."

"No. Let's check the other end of the hallway."

I tried to keep up as he rushed down the long hall to the other end where a glass door blocked access to a stairwell. He pushed the door open, and I barely had time to slip through before it swinged close again.

Running down the stairs was only marginally easier than running up them. I wouldn't need a spin class tonight.

Luca burst through a door at the bottom of the stairs, and I hurried to catch up. There was a pedestrian tunnel outside the door, connecting two shopping streets, and our sudden appearance made people give us baffled looks. Luca ignored them and just ran to the street outside the restaurant, only to stop.

I reached him and together we stared after the retreating form of a white Fiat 500 that we'd seen less than two hours earlier outside Finch's house. Shepard was in the backseat, his head lolling against the window. Finch was in the passenger seat, and behind the wheel—was Danielle.

"What do we do now?" I asked. Upset was driving the excellent meal back up—or it could be the mad rush we'd just done.

"We need to tell Kane."

I'd sort of hoped to avoid it, but if Danielle was involved in kidnapping people, he needed to know. I took out my phone and, reluctantly, placed the call to Kane.

"Phoebe? Are you still at the museum?"

I'd forgotten how innocently the day had begun. "No. Something's come up and we need your help. Can you contact Hunt for us? And maybe come over too to meet with him?"

"Can it wait?"

I sighed. "Not really. In fact, the sooner we act, the better."

Third Spell's the Charm

"What's happened?" He sounded concerned now.

"I'd rather not explain it on the phone. Just let us know if you can reach Hunt. If not, we'll have to do without him."

"I'll see what I can do." He hung up, and we had an agonizing five minutes to wait until he called back. "You're in luck. He's at the gay club we met in earlier. Can you meet him there?"

"Yes, we're close. We'll wait for you outside."

We headed to the club. Part of me wanted to hurry so that we could save Shepard, but part of me dreaded the conversations we were about to have, with Kane and Hunt both.

Kane arrived in a taxi soon after we'd reached the club. It wasn't open yet, so we headed to the back door, which opened before we had a chance to press the buzzer.

Ronnie greeted us with a curious look, but he didn't ask questions as he guided us to a small office, where Hunt was waiting, sitting behind a neat desk. He gave us an impatient frown.

"This had better be good."

Kane took a seat at the only guest chair after I'd declined, and Luca and I glanced at each other. I nodded at him to talk, but he shook his head. "This is your show."

I didn't agree, but Hunt didn't look like he'd listen to our dithering much longer. I drew a fortifying breath, wishing I'd accepted the seat after all.

"The short story is that we witnessed Adam Finch kidnap Maxim Shepard just now."

"What? Why?" Hunt demanded. I spread my arms, out of words.

"I … have no idea. We can only presume that Finch is the vampire we're after."

"I told you, it's not him," Hunt stated.

"Then why did he kidnap Shepard?"

"Wasn't Finch the ex-boyfriend of Miss Peaches?" Kane asked, and when I nodded he scratched his jaw, thinking. "Maybe it's personal. Maybe he holds Shepard responsible for her death?"

It sounded plausible. "Kidnapping is a bit excessive though. And it only works if he isn't the killer we're after."

"He isn't. I already told you," Hunt huffed, getting up. "So I don't see why we, or I, should get involved."

"Other than it's the decent thing to do?" But he only stared down at me from his superior height, so I continued. "Because he wasn't acting alone."

I looked at Kane, my stomach tightening painfully in dread for his reaction. "Danielle is back. And she was driving the car."

Thirteen

KANE'S FACE TURNED INTO A tight mask. "I see."

"Who's Danielle?" Hunt asked. I glanced at Kane, but he didn't seem inclined to contribute.

"Kane's ex-wife. She's chosen the dark side of magic. She's dating a warlock, and who knows where that path will lead her."

"But to kidnapping?" Kane huffed, finding his voice.

"That's not the only thing she's done for Finch," Luca said. "She was at his house earlier, warding it."

"What for?"

Luca spread his arms. "At a guess, to keep Shepard from fleeing."

I turned at him, stunned. "That didn't even occur to me. That's where they'll be. We have to go after them, right now."

"I still don't understand why I need to be involved," Hunt drawled. I pulled straight, too incensed to guard my words.

"Because Finch is a more powerful vampire than you've led us believe. You knew him already a century ago. I don't know how he's convinced you he's not the vampire we're after, but I'm not willing to ignore that possibility."

His face twisted into a snarl. "Did you go looking into my past?" His power rose, pressing on me, making it difficult to breathe, let alone speak, but I managed to nod.

"You're the key to this, whether you want to be or not. I don't know why you're so afraid of what we might find. So far, there's only been admirable things. Like the Tube line you built with Finch."

The pressure on me cut abruptly. "You found about that?"

"There are newspaper articles," I said, exasperated. "It wasn't even difficult."

It had been, a little, but I wouldn't admit to it aloud.

"Can't we at least try to save Shepard?" I'd hate to see another innocent human die at the hands of a vampire if I could do something about it.

"I'll deal with it," Hunt stated, rounding the desk. Kane rose too.

"You can't go after him alone if he's teamed with Danielle. You'll need a mage's help."

Hunt shot him a glare over his shoulder, then looked at Luca and me. "And I guess you want to attend too?"

Want wasn't the correct word, but we nodded.

"Come on, then."

He ordered Ronnie, who was waiting in the hallway, to follow us, and soon we found ourselves in a Land Rover even larger than Ashley's, with Ronnie driving and Hunt in the front seat. I had the middle seat at the back, which would have been a comfortable spot if Kane hadn't been so rigidly angry next to me. I was almost certain he wasn't angry with *me*, but it didn't help much.

Third Spell's the Charm

The evening rush hadn't started yet, so we made good time across the river. But traffic began to drag as we passed Waterloo Station, and came to a complete standstill at the roundabout on its north side. A police vehicle was blocking the street we meant to take, and lights of emergency vehicles were blinking in the distance.

"I don't like this," Hunt stated. He opened the door. "We'll walk from here. You take the car where you can and wait for us there," he ordered Ronnie.

We followed him past the police blockade. They didn't try to stop us, so whatever the emergency was, we weren't in immediate danger because of it.

There were no roadblocks on the next street, but as the emergency vehicles increased, it became obvious that we were walking towards the hub of the disaster.

"Maybe it's the pub at the corner of Finch's street," I suggested, when I spotted a barricade outside it.

We reached the barricade and didn't need to go farther. The narrow street Finch lived on was blocked with fire engines, and they were hosing down a very familiar house.

"This can't be good..." Luca muttered.

"Not with that many fire engines putting down the fire," Kane said grimly.

"Do you think the house was empty?" My stomach roiled with the idea that people could have been inside.

Not just any people. Finch, Shepard, and Danielle.

I glanced at Kane, but his face was unreadable. We stood there with half the neighbourhood staring at the scene, watching the firefighters gain control of the fire slowly but steadily.

"This is an odd fire," Hunt noted after a while, the first words he'd spoken since we left the car. "There's barely any smoke and it's contained to Finch's house even though it's attached to other houses on both sides."

Now that he mentioned it, I didn't even smell smoke. "What does that mean?"

"Good question. We need to investigate."

Ronnie showed up, having become bored with waiting. I realised we'd been standing there for an hour already. "I spoke to my dad. The fire's out, but they're going to stay and make sure it's completely extinguished."

"Is Ashley there too?" I asked, a new worry adding to the old one.

He flashed a brief smile. "Yes, but don't worry, she's an experienced lass and she said it wasn't a dangerous job."

Kane cleared his throat, swallowing hard. "Have they found ... any bodies?"

Ronnie gave him a grim nod. "One. But they don't know whose. It's ... too badly burned."

The remains of my lunch threatened to come up.

"Do you think they brought Shepard here and set the place on fire?" Luca asked, his eyes growing large with horror.

"That's one explanation," Hunt said, amazingly calmly, as if he weren't talking about a brutal murder.

"What other explanations could there possibly be?" My voice rose to about an octave higher than normal. He gave me a level look.

"That the body is wholly unrelated, someone Finch is using to fake his own death."

I was ashamed to confess how relieved that made me.

"Then where are they?" Kane asked, his hair billowing as if preparing to smite someone with magic. I wanted to put a hand on his arm and assure him Danielle was all right, but since my confidence was based on the old adage that nothing killed evil, I kept my mouth shut.

"Why don't you call her," Luca suggested. Kane startled.

"What?"

"Danielle. You have her phone number, don't you?"

Kane took out his phone and stared at it as if he'd never seen it before. He opened it, selected Danielle's number, and placed the call. He waited for a long time, but she didn't answer. It didn't calm him.

"Where is she?" he growled.

"Her house?" I suggested, the only place I could come up with.

He pulled back. "Why would she keep it, if she lives in France?"

I didn't find it at all odd. "She's dating a warlock she left once already. Maybe she wants to keep her own place as insurance."

Hunt made an impatient gesture. "Either we let them go and wash our hands of this business, or we go check her house. It's the only lead we have, and we can't go chasing around aimlessly, hoping for a break."

Since no one had any objections, and we couldn't just stand there watching the firefighters work, we followed Ronnie to where he'd left the car.

DANIELLE LIVED—or had lived, at least—about five miles upriver in Fulham, near Hurlingham Park where the elite players played rugby and polo. Or so Luca had informed me when we were there the first time. We had trailed Danielle there, only to be chased away by a hellhound to said park. It would've eaten us if Ashley hadn't come to our rescue in her wolf form and killed it.

Good times.

Ronnie pulled over by the street and we sat in the car, assessing the place for threats. Danielle's house was a large redbrick at the corner of two streets. The rooms facing the streets were dark, but we couldn't see the rear windows from where we were.

"Are we all needed there?" Hunt asked, eyeing the place dubiously. If it hadn't been for the hellhound incident, I would've said the house with its overgrown hedges looked charming and harmless. Now I just nodded as I exited the car.

"Definitely."

"Her car isn't here," Luca noted, studying the vehicles parked by the street. I wasn't discouraged.

"Maybe it's in the back yard." There was a small space behind the house for a car, the gate so covered with hedges it was barely visible.

Luca sprinted there to take a look. "It's here," he said when he returned. "So she definitely lives here. How are we handling this?"

"We can't just march up to the door and demand Danielle release the prisoner," I said. "Can we?"

"We don't even know if Finch and Shepard are here," Kane said. "She could've been just the driver."

"Nevertheless, she'll know where they are," Hunt stated. Luca nodded.

"We'd best not go in blindly. I'll sneak in to look through the back."

I'd witnessed him scale Danielle's walls like a spider—or Spider-Man—and although he'd done it without incidents, I gave him a worried look. "You'll need someone to watch your back."

Third Spell's the Charm

I was about to volunteer, even though the memory of the hellhound still turned my bones liquid, when Ronnie nodded.

"I'll stand guard."

"Watch out for hellhounds," I told him, and his eyes flashed with excitement.

"I'm looking forward to seeing one. I can't let my sister be better than me."

I shuddered with fear, and he grinned as he headed down the street after Luca to slip into the back garden. It was getting dark, but the neighbours would spot them if they weren't careful. And if Danielle was home, she might spot them too.

"We need a distraction."

Hunt sneered. "Archibald showing up at her door should be a distraction enough."

Kane rolled his eyes, but headed to the front door, Hunt and I trailing him. He pressed the doorbell and it chimed inside. Nothing happened, and I gave Hunt a questioning look. He narrowed his eyes, listening.

"I can't hear anything. Is there a basement? Maybe they're there."

"Maybe she's just ignoring the bell."

Kane rang the doorbell again. This time footsteps approached the door and we tensed. But when the door opened, it was only Luca.

"The house is empty."

We filed in. I looked around curiously, eager to see if Danielle's tastes were similar to Kane's, who had appointed his home in mid-century modern style. But she preferred traditional English décor with stuffed upholstery and Laura Ashley wallpaper; pretty, but unremarkable.

While I was admiring the interior, the men spread around the house to make sure it was truly empty. There was no basement, and even though there were several rooms, no one was hiding in them.

We gathered at the sitting room by the front door. Kane shook his head. "She's not here and we have no more leads. We'd better leave."

"Shouldn't one of us stay in case she returns?" I asked. Ronnie sighed.

"I'll stay. But there had better be hellhounds showing up."

"That can be arranged," a male voice drawled from the hallway.

STARTLED, I SWIVELLED around to look. No one had entered through the front door and the place had definitely been empty a moment ago. My skin tightened in fear when I saw who it was.

Laurent Dufort, warlock and Danielle's partner, was looming in the doorway, filling it with his tall and powerfully built frame, a threatening sight in black trousers and black silk shirt. He looked to be in his early forties, but he could be over a hundred years old. His elegantly cut black hair had some grey at the temples, and his nose was hooked and very French.

Magical energy crackled around him like static electricity, brushing against my skin uncomfortably, and his starkly handsome face was distorted with a furious glower.

His dark eyes were burning. "What are you doing here?"

He spotted Kane and lifted his hand in front of him, as if about to cast a spell. The men around me instantly

Third Spell's the Charm

prepared for an attack and a low growl filled the small room.

"Stop!" I said, sounding braver than I was. "We need him if we want to find Danielle."

His gaze landed on me, its strength making my knees buckle. Hunt had nothing on the fury of a warlock.

"Danielle is missing?" His French accent turned more pronounced. "What is this?"

"That's what we're here to find out," Kane answered, sounding calm and in control once more. He lowered his hand, and his hair stopped billowing. "I'm afraid she was involved in ... an incident."

Everyone looked at me, as if it were my duty to tell the already enraged warlock what his girlfriend had done. But since I didn't want to appear a coward, I took a fortifying breath and plunged in.

"We encountered her earlier when she was leaving a house she said she had been warding. Two hours later, we witnessed her helping the vampire whose house she had warded to kidnap a man. A little after that, the warded house burned down. One body was found, and since we had no other leads, we came here to see if she was home. She isn't, although her car is. She's not answering her phone. We have no idea what has become of her, or where she and the vampire might be, but it's not looking good."

Dufort stared at me for a few scary heartbeats that made me wish I'd used Danielle's loo when we arrived. Then his face distorted with anger, and he cursed heavily in French. It made my ears burn and I wasn't a prude.

"She was supposed to handle the wards for the vampire, that is all," he said, after he calmed down enough to speak. "Then she was to return here and I was to fetch her home."

That would explain why, and how, he was here. He could create portals that bridged vast distances. He'd come to my aid once when Kane was unconscious after a spell backfired, stepping out of thin air as if he'd been in the next room instead of France.

He dug out a phone from the pocket of his trousers, the mundane act at odds with what he was, though I guess even warlocks had to keep up with the times. He placed a call, and a ringtone chimed behind me.

As one, we twirled to the sound, but she hadn't miraculously materialised behind us. Luca cocked his head and followed the sound to the sofa. He crouched and reached under it, pulling out the phone.

"She wouldn't have left this behind."

"You must find her!" Dufort ordered, putting his phone away.

Kane crossed arms over his chest, studying Dufort calmly. "Why would we do that?"

Dufort's eyes narrowed, and the crackling of static electricity returned. "Because I saved your life and you owe me."

Kane's brows furrowed, but he couldn't deny the truth. "We have nothing to work with."

Dufort gestured widely. "This is her home. There are plenty of personal things here for you to use for tracing her."

Kane dipped his chin. "In that case, I need your assistance."

"Of course you do," Dufort sneered. He turned his attention to us. "But first, who the hell are you people?"

Fourteen

LIKE ANY GOOD MAGE—or evil—Danielle had a room upstairs dedicated to spell work. It had a bare, easily cleanable wooden floor, and wooden shelves at one end holding everything a self-respecting mage could need. It was well-stocked and dust-free, as was the house, come to think of it.

We all followed Dufort there, everyone curious to see what would happen, even Hunt. Maybe he hadn't often had a chance to witness mages cast spells.

It had been interesting to watch Hunt and Dufort make each other's acquaintance. They'd both pulled straight and measured one another for power and—it seemed—age too. I was almost certain Hunt was the older, but equally sure that Dufort was more powerful.

Dufort went about the shelves like he knew the place well, another indication that the pair spent more time here than we'd assumed. He found a piece of chalk and a detailed map of London. He gave the first to Kane.

"You draw. My special ... skills might interfere with the pattern."

Kane didn't argue but drew a complex pattern on the floor without needing to consult a book. He'd done this before. I'd witnessed it even, and had been greatly impressed.

"Isn't this a three-mage spell?" I watched him closely, trying to memorise the pattern.

Dufort smirked. "Are you volunteering to participate, little mage?" I stepped hastily back, and the smirk turned to sneer. "I'm powerful enough to handle the part of two mages."

"But what sort of power is it?" Kane asked, straightening. Dufort cocked a brow.

"The kind that gets the job done."

Judging by the tightness of Kane's jaw, it didn't sit well with him that he had to resort to the warlock's help, but it would've taken too long to get Giselle and Amber here to help. So he simply finished drawing the pattern and then took his place on it.

Dufort spread the map on the floor inside the circle. Then he pulled out a pendant from around his neck that turned out to be a tiny vial with red liquid inside it.

My gut roiled when I realised it had to be Danielle's blood. That wasn't creepy at all.

He placed the vial on the map and then looked at me. "The spell still needs a third mage to prevent the energy from bleeding away. Step in."

Kane stiffened. "Absolutely not! She's not strong enough."

Dufort tilted his head, studying me with narrowed eyes. "I think she's very strong."

I didn't know what to think of his praise, but I shook my head. "I can't even manage a basic water spell."

"No one asks you to cast any spells. Just to hold the energy inside the circle."

Third Spell's the Charm

"Maybe I can be of assistance?" Hunt said, but Dufort lifted a hand in front of him, stopping him.

"I need a mage. Your magic is ... the wrong kind."

"As if yours is so right..." Kane muttered, but Dufort ignored him and just pointed at the correct spot.

"In."

I cast a hesitant glance at Kane, who nodded. A shiver of anticipation and fear ran down my spine as I stepped to the correct spot.

"Empty your mind and concentrate on the spark of magic inside you," Kane instructed me. "And when the energy starts to build, let it pass through you into the circle."

I shook my shoulders and tried to relax. It was impossible to completely shut out the people around me, but I tried my best. Finding the spark was easy enough and I nodded at the mages. As if on cue, they began to chant.

At first, I didn't sense anything. But little by little, as the energy was drawn into the circle and made to multiply, my body began to react to it. It vibrated minutely and then stronger and stronger until my entire body was buzzing like in an electric storm.

It was uncomfortable and then downright painful, my skin prickling like a million needless hitting it at once. Power began to press me until it was difficult to breathe. I grit my jaws together, determined to ride the storm, but I was finding it difficult to even stay upright. And still the chanting continued, drawing in more energy.

I heard Hunt's voice somewhere behind me. "You're meant to release the energy, Phoebe, not to hoard it."

"I. Don't. Know. How." It hurt to speak.

"Just let go."

And I did, mostly because I was out of choices. The energy released at once, deflating me, almost making me drop on my knees.

The incantation changed. Instead of gathering the energy, Kane and Dufort were directing it to the spell they were casting. The vial began to float over the map. I tried to sense what they were doing, but I couldn't follow the currents.

Abruptly, it stopped. The energy disappeared completely, leaving me oddly empty and cold. The vial dropped on the map, the edge of its stopper pointing at a specific location. Kane and Dufort leaned down to look, but I was too tired to make the effort.

Kane cursed.

Hearing a foul word from him was such a shock that it forced me to step closer and look too. At first I didn't understand what had upset him. When I did, I wanted to curse too.

"What's wrong?" Dufort asked.

"That's Finch's house," I told him, my voice hoarse as if I'd been shouting. "The house that burned down."

If Danielle was there, she couldn't possibly be alive.

"No!" Dufort made a slashing motion with his hand. "There must be a mistake."

Kane looked grim. "We'd best go and see ourselves."

I wasn't looking forward to that, but we had to be sure. He and Dufort stepped out of the circle. I made to follow when Kane halted me.

"You have to release the excess energy."

"I already did."

"There's always some build-up, and you hoarded quite a lot of it. Only a small spell is needed to release it; a wind or water spell will do."

Third Spell's the Charm

I cast the wind spell he had taught me, the gestures perfect, the incantation clear in my mind.

The map burst on fire.

Kane and Dufort jumped back, but I was too tired to even react. Kane quickly doused the fire, but the map had already turned to ash. Tears sprang to my eyes, mostly for exhaustion, but for embarrassment too.

"I'm sorry."

Kane gave me a consoling smile. "Don't worry about it. It's my fault. I forgot that this might happen."

Dufort studied me with interest. "Why did your wind spell cause fire?"

"Every spell I cast creates fire," I said miserably. His brows shot up, but instead of laughing he tilted his head.

"Fascinating. You should look into that."

"Of course…"

I was too tired to care. I hadn't even cast the spell myself—the accidental fire didn't count—and my every muscle ached like I'd run a marathon after staying up all night.

Listlessly, I headed downstairs with my companions. Luca wrapped an arm around me, and I leaned against him. It was either that or fall on my face.

Ronnie gave the car keys to Hunt. "I'll stay here to guard the house. Maybe the hellhound returns."

Dufort sneered. "I can summon one for you, if you like."

"On second thought, I'll pass."

THE MOMENT I WAS in the car I fell asleep. I only realised I'd been leaning against Kane's shoulder when he woke me up. I was too tired to be embarrassed.

The fire engines and barricades blocking Finch's street were gone, but the entrance to his house was barred with a barrier. There were only holes where the door and windows had been. Even the three windows above them were gone.

A uniformed police officer stood guard. We paused a little way away to gawp, but the officer didn't pay us any heed.

"Wow!" Luca said after a while. "That place is *gone*."

The walls were blackened with smoke, but amazingly that was as far as it went. "The neighbours escaped the worst though. Even their windows are still intact."

I wasn't an expert on housefires, but I'd seen pictures in newspapers, and the heat usually blew out the windows near the fire. On a narrow street like this, the windows across the street should have suffered some heat damage too.

Kane studied the house with his head tilted. "That is … interesting. I take it Danielle's wards were meant to keep the fire from spreading?" He glanced at Dufort, who made a very Gallic shrug.

"I have no idea. But she creates excellent wards."

"Let's go take a look," Hunt said. He walked forward without waiting for us. I was reluctant to go closer, but I was the only one.

Had it been up to me to gain access into the house, I would've asked the police officer nicely, then a bit more firmly when he inevitably refused, and still I probably would've been denied access. Hunt walked up to him, and when he turned to look he mesmerised the man. The officer's eyes glazed over.

"It won't hold long, so we have to be fast."

Third Spell's the Charm

It was dark already, the street was empty, and no one was peering through curtains when we pushed past the barriers and entered the husk of a house. I paused on the threshold. It wasn't as hot in there as I'd feared, but the floor was a wet wreck, squelching and swaying under every step the men took. Moreover, I was wearing a very nice pair of boots that would be ruined.

My mouth dropped open as I took in the wreck. Everything inside was gone, the walls between rooms and the upper floors all the way to the rafters in the attic. Curiously though, the wooden beams and the roof were intact.

The house was an empty shell between its outer walls. Two chimneys made of brick stood in the middle of the space like columns, the fireplaces they had connected to only piles of brick on the floor. Not even a hint of furniture remained, and the kitchen fixtures were a molten mess. A bomb or napalm couldn't have done this kind of damage.

I stepped inside and a bitter stench of burned, soaked wood assaulted my sinuses. I coughed, gasping for fresh air.

"It didn't smell this bad outside."

Kane and Dufort looked around. "It's the wards," Dufort stated.

"You mean they weren't damaged in the fire?" Kane asked, his eyes narrowing as he studied the walls.

He gestured with his hands and fingers, and I sensed the energy of a spell rise. I'd witnessed him cast this particular spell before, but the effects weren't as dramatic this time round.

A faint glow appeared on the front wall. If the wards were intact, they were under the soot. Kane leaned closer and studied them carefully.

"They're too unclear to tell what these are supposed to do."

Dufort came to look too. "It's definitely Danielle's work."

He went to the wall adjoining the neighbour's and cast the same spell Kane had. More wards began to glow faintly under the soot.

Kane gestured at them. "I think it's safe to assume that she's warded this place so that the fire didn't spread from this house to the neighbours."

"And she succeeded," Hunt said. "But how do you create a fire this destructive?"

He sounded like it was more than idle curiosity. Maybe he was already planning his next exit in a blaze of glory.

Dufort gave him a proud look. "My spell. I created it during a war once. I had no idea Danielle had learned it this well."

Taking pride in destruction was probably normal for a warlock—or maybe it was the pride of a teacher.

I frowned. "How do you destroy the place this completely without destroying the body? Shouldn't it have burned with the rest?"

Dufort dipped his chin. "My Danielle is brilliant with wards."

"You mean she warded the body so that it didn't burn too badly?"

"Or it was burned already and planted here inside the protective wards," he suggested.

Hunt nodded. "I think this is Finch faking his death and not a murder scene."

Third Spell's the Charm

"But it doesn't explain why Danielle is here?" Dufort said, but Kane shook his head.

"She can't be here. There's nowhere to hide."

"She might not be hiding. Maybe she's in the back garden," Luca suggested.

I wasn't willing to cross the floor to the gaping hole where the back door had been, but I followed the others, holding my breath in case it made me lighter. The floor held.

The small garden was as undamaged by fire as everything outside the wards, but soaked with water. The air was fresher again the moment I escaped the house, and I took deep gulps.

Tall brick walls separated the garden from its neighbours, and a brick shed lined the bottom towards the next street over. Steps led down to a cellar.

Hunt studied them. "Could she have warded the cellar to withstand the fire?"

"Yes," Dufort stated, taking the steps down. He checked the door for wards, and a simple lock spell showed up. He disarmed it and pushed the door open.

It was dark inside, so he created a ball of light and sent it in, following right behind it. Kane and Hunt went in too, but I refused to go under a house that might collapse on me at any moment, no matter how great Danielle's wards were.

When the men didn't immediately emerge with news about the contents of the cellar, good or bad, and they didn't sound like they needed help from an inept mage and a vampire, I began to relax. Luca pointed at the shed.

"Let's go check that."

Since it was the only other place where anyone could be, we crossed the soggy garden there. Like all the doors on the street, the door was wooden and painted brightly to contrast with the dour walls, red in this case. Luca made to reach for the handle, but I placed a hand on his forearm to halt him.

"What if there's a ward on it too?"

He shot me a hopeful look. "Can't you check?"

I huffed. "I'm not Kane. I'm not even a proper mage."

I had watched carefully how he made the wards appear. It wasn't complicated, but I only knew the hand movements. If there was a silent incantation, I could wave my hands all I wanted and the spell wouldn't catch.

Let's face it, even if I knew the whole spell, nothing would happen. And I was exhausted to boot.

"The mages are busy in the cellar. Give it a try."

His impish grin made me smile and shrug. It wouldn't hurt to wave my hands around. I concentrated like I'd been taught and gathered the spark inside me. It came surprisingly easy, considering how exhausted I was. I traced the hand movements I'd witnessed Kane to do.

The door burst on fire.

My startled shriek brought Kane to us in leaps across the garden. He doused the fire with a quick spell, shaking his head.

"At least you didn't burn your hair this time…"

I stared at the door miserably. It hadn't burned badly, only the paint had singed, but who knows what would've happened if Kane hadn't been here.

Luca was laughing so hard he had trouble breathing. I punched him in the arm, but it only made him laugh more.

"What were you trying to do this time?" Kane asked. He wasn't laughing, but his eyes were twinkling.

"I wanted to check if the door is warded," I said, more grumpily than I intended.

Third Spell's the Charm

He patted me on the shoulder. "It was a good attempt, if you managed this."

"Hardly..." But his praise lifted my spirits a little.

Dufort and Hunt crossed the garden to us. "What happened?"

"Phoebe set the door on fire," Luca said with a guffaw. Hunt looked puzzled, and Dufort intrigued, but neither said anything to my relief.

Kane made the wards appear on the door with the same economic moves as earlier. No fire.

Dufort broke the wards and pulled the door open with an impatient tug. The place was empty. His shoulders slumped minutely, and I was actually sorry for him. Evil warlock or no, he was truly worried for Danielle.

The shed turned out to be a garage with no car in it. Double doors opened to the next street over. Dufort stared at the empty space, magical energy crackling for his anger.

"Where is Danielle?"

There was nothing inside to hide behind or in. She wasn't here.

Hunt closed the door. "I think it's time to check who is at the morgue."

Fifteen

IF THERE WAS ONE PLACE I never wanted to end up in—at least while still alive—it was a morgue. I certainly hadn't planned to visit one tonight.

St Thomas's was so close I didn't have time to come up with an excuse to stay in the car. Far too soon, I found myself following a vampire, a mage, and a warlock into a morgue.

That was not an opening of a joke. Besides, there were two vampires, but Luca was hanging back with me.

A hospital this large never closed, most assuredly not in a busy city like London, but that didn't include the morgue. The door was locked and the lights in the hallway behind the glass pane of the door were switched off.

"Oh well, we'll have to come another day," I said, feigning disappointment, ready to head back to the car.

Hunt didn't bother to answer me. He merely made a simple hand gesture much like a mage's and pulled the door open. He went in first and switched off the alarm with magic so fast that he had to have known where it was.

"Do you come here often?" I quipped to hide my nervousness. It was one thing to visit a morgue. Breaking into one was beyond my paygrade.

He gave me a calm look. "Yes. This is the most logical place to leave bodies."

Okay…

"Won't the people working here start asking questions if unidentified bodies show up?"

He shrugged. "Not if you do it right."

He walked down the hallway and the lights switched on automatically. It smelled of hospital, which wasn't my favourite scent, but better than dead bodies. I glanced back nervously. No one was around, and the exit was shielded by a hedge lining the parking lot, so no one could spot the hallway lights from the outside.

"You dump the bodies into the morgue?" Kane asked, appalled.

"When it's more convenient. Sometimes I use the hospital incinerator."

Kane and I shared an incredulous look behind Hunt's back. Dufort sneered. Luca patted my shoulder.

"Aren't you glad I don't kill my food?"

"Emphatically yes."

Hunt shot a look over his shoulder. "I haven't killed my food in decades either."

"Then why am I still ostracised?" Luca asked, incensed.

"It still isn't a popular position. Not everyone is strong enough to manage it."

Then where did the bodies he left here come from? Did he handle the victims of other vampires too? Or do some recreational killing outside feeding? He was a

Third Spell's the Charm

businessman. Maybe he got rid of the competition, permanently.

He turned to another hallway deeper into the hospital and the lights came on there as well. It was eerily silent, only some machines were humming. I walked as silently as I could, my back stiff, fearing someone would show up at any moment demanding to know what we were doing there.

I was so focused on it that I didn't even notice I'd followed Hunt into the autopsy theatre until the drop in temperature alerted me. I halted abruptly, but the door closed behind me before I could flee.

Just the same. I wouldn't have been brave enough to stay in the hallway alone anyway.

The room looked pretty much like those on TV: pale green walls, a worn, grey-green tile floor, and a lot of steel fixtures. Everything was clean and neatly in its place, and it smelled strongly of disinfectant and not at all of blood—or worse things.

There wasn't a dead body in sight.

"Let's see…" Hunt went to a computer at a desk closest to the door. He moved the mouse and the screen came to life.

"The thing about morgues is that no one ever remembers to log off…"

That would explain how he could hide bodies here without rousing suspicions. He made a quick search and then crossed the room to swinging double doors at the other end.

"The bodies are kept here."

Kane, Dufort, and Luca followed him, and since I didn't want to be left alone, I did too.

That room was even colder, and a loud hum of cooling units filled the space. The long walls on both sides of the door had body-sized steel hatches side by side in four rows on top of one another. At a quick glance, you could fit almost a hundred bodies here.

Hunt headed to one of the hatches and opened it. I stiffened when he pulled the gurney out of the freezer, but the body was covered with a green sheet. Then he pulled it off.

I surged to the bin by the door.

Leaning over it, I pinched my eyes closed and held my breath to keep the contents of my stomach in. The impassive tone with which Hunt described the body did not help. Kane and Dufort participated too, as if they weren't affected by the charred remains.

I only began to pay attention when Hunt said the word human. "Definitely not a vampire."

"Not Danielle either," Dufort stated. "Too tall."

"So Finch did fake his own death?" Luca asked.

"It could be Shepard."

I didn't dare to open my mouth to contribute, in case I tasted the body in the air. I kept myself rigid until I heard the gurney being pushed back inside the freezer and the door closing.

A warm hand landed on my shoulder. "You can open your eyes now, Phoebe," Kane said. He sounded concerned instead of amused, which threated to bring tears to my eyes. I was far beyond my comfort zone here.

"Can we go now?"

"Absolutely."

He offered me his arm and I accepted it gratefully, boss or not. He tended to behave less like a boss when we

Third Spell's the Charm

were on a magic-related venture anyway. We retreated to the autopsy theatre.

"Can I wash my hands before we go?" I hadn't touched anything, but I was convinced germs were crawling all over me. I would've needed a glass of water too to wash off the bile that kept rising to my mouth, but even though I knew the water was perfectly normal and safe, I couldn't bring myself to drink it.

I wetted a paper towel and wiped my neck with it. It revived me enough to face the room again, but I had to lean my backside against the sink to stay up.

"What do we do now?"

"Danielle hasn't returned home," Dufort said, his voice tight with genuine worry. "But I'm not familiar with this Finch person to know where he would take her."

We turned to Hunt, who pulled back. "What?"

"You're the only one who knows him," Luca said.

"It was over a century ago," Hunt said, aggravated. "I've barely seen the man since."

"Back to the research it is, then," I sighed, pushing up.

I was more than ready to leave, but my legs had different ideas. I steeled them, determined to walk out on my own and not lean for a man's arm for support, even if the man was Kane.

I braced myself for the first step when a strange noise from the freezer room startled me, wiping away what the steel I'd mustered.

"Do you hear that?"

The vampires were instantly alert, their hearing better than mine. Luca nodded. "It's as if someone is banging the doors in the freezer."

"That's not funny."

"Maybe it's the pipes," Kane suggested. Luca grinned at me.

"Let's go look."

"Absolutely not!"

"If you don't see for yourself that there's nothing there, you'll have nightmares for months."

Since he was right, I allowed him to drag me to the freezer. He paused in the middle of the room to listen. The banging was much clearer here.

I inhaled in shock. "There's someone trapped inside!"

Hunt muttered a curse and crossed the floor to the source of the sound. We followed, some of us more reluctantly than others.

Me. I was the reluctant one.

Hunt chose a door without hesitation, as if knowing already what was going on, opened it, and pulled out the gurney.

The body on it shot to sitting up with a shriek and flaying arms, and my body turned cold in shock.

"Let me out, let me out!"

"You are out," Hunt said calmly, and the person turned to him.

I got a good look at their face and my legs ceased from supporting me. Dropping on my knees, I stared at Miss Peaches with my mouth hanging open.

"Phoebe, is that you? Where am I? Oh my God, is this a morgue? Is this some kind of a joke? Because you didn't seem like a joking kind of a woman."

Miss Peaches's questions washed over me, her voice getting higher as the freakout got worse. I leaned slowly down until my forehead rested on the cold tiles, unheeding of the germs there might be. I closed my eyes so that I didn't have to watch black spots dance on the sick green of the tiles.

Kane crouched by me, his hand on my back, gently rubbing between my shoulder blades, while Luca tried to calm Miss Peaches.

"Hey, Miss Peaches," he said in a calming tone I barely recognised coming out of his mouth. "Or do you prefer Sam?"

"How do you know that name?"

"We had to find out. You see..." He drew a fortifying breath. "You died."

"I what?" There was a scrambling sound. "I need to get out of here."

"Easy," Luca said, followed by a heavy thump that sounded like a grown man dropping on the floor unconscious.

"Why did you do that for?" Luca asked, sounding like his normal self.

"He was spiralling out," Hunt said calmly. "Time for that is later. We need to leave before security comes. Can Phoebe walk?"

A warm hand parted the veil of hair covering my face. Kane's concerned eyes studied me. "Are you able to get up, or shall I cast a tiny spell that'll steady you for a moment."

"Will it burn my hair?"

He chuckled. "No."

I was tempted to give him the go-ahead, but I gritted my teeth and pushed myself up to sit on my knees. I looked around carefully, but the dizziness was gone. Hunt and Luca had lifted Miss Peaches's unconscious body onto a gurney and were already wheeling her out of the freezer, Dufort at their heels, a bemused look on his face.

I had a fair notion he wasn't bemused often.

Kane's arm steadying me around my waist, I stood up. My legs held, so I pulled myself straight, tugged my clothes into place, and stepped away from Kane to preserve what dignity I had left. Which, after two accidental fires and near fainting, wasn't much.

"Thank you. I think I can manage."

My legs were tottery, but they held all the way out of the building. Luca drove Ronnie's car to the door, and shielded by the hedge, he and Hunt manoeuvred the unconscious Miss Peaches into the back seat.

"I don't think there's room for all of us," Luca noted, closing the car door. "You take the car. Phoebe and I will take a taxi home."

No one tried to suggest we keep on searching for Danielle, not even Dufort.

Kane shot us a concerned look, but he didn't object. He took the car keys from Luca and sat behind the wheel. Hunt took the back seat, likely to keep an eye on the newly awoken vampire, and Dufort the front.

We watched the car drive away. Then Luca wrapped an arm around my shoulders. "Let's head to the front entrance. There's bound to be taxis outside A&E, no matter what time of night it is."

He was right.

We didn't speak a word on our way home, and the driver was mercifully quiet too, though I could see from the curious looks he gave us through the rear-view mirror that he was dying to know what kind of an accident had brought us to the A&E smelling of smoke and looking like we'd seen a ghost.

The cab left us outside the magic shop, and since it was still open to serve customers who couldn't face daylight—or didn't want to—we went in through it. Amber took one look at us and pointed upstairs.

"Kitchen."

She went to close the shop and followed us before we'd managed to climb all the way up. Giselle was knitting in front of the TV, but she switched it off when she noticed us and hurried to the kitchen. Soon we were sitting around the large oak table, sipping Giselle's calming tea.

Then the questions began. We tried to answer the best we could, but I don't know if we made any sense. It was a long tale, starting from meeting Danielle at Finch's house, the kidnapping, the fire, Danielle missing, and searching for her with Dufort's help. I was already on my second cup of tea before we reached the morgue.

I was reluctant to speak about it, so Luca told the rest: "We went to the morgue to see who the body found in the fire belonged to. Hunt was fairly sure it was a human and probably male, so not Danielle." He inhaled deeply, searching for words.

"And then we found Miss Peaches."

"The person who was killed at the club?" Amber asked. "Hunt brought her there?"

Luca took a sip of tea. "It's the best place to stash a body to wait for it to wake up. And she did."

"What?" The women shrieked in unison.

"Are you saying Miss Peaches came back from the dead?" Giselle asked, her face pale. "While you were in there?"

"Yep."

"Oh, poor Phoebe. No wonder you look like you've seen a ghost." She pulled me into an herb scented hug. It was wonderfully restorative.

"So Miss Peaches is a vampire now?" Amber asked.

"Yes."

She frowned. "Without her permission?"

Luca spread his arms. "Most of us are made without consent. Most of us are from eras when the word, let alone the idea, didn't even exist, so it doesn't occur to us that consent is needed. I'm not saying it's right, but sometimes it beats being dead."

"What if Miss Peaches doesn't want to be a vampire?" Giselle asked. He gave her an assuring look.

"There are ways to … undo what's been done. And this time with consent."

"So who did it?"

I stared at my tea, trying to fish out threads that were hiding inside my tired brain. "It had to be Finch. The reason he and Miss Peaches broke up was because he couldn't tell her he's a vampire. And now she is one too."

Luca shook his head. "It's a good theory, but…" He hesitated. "I'm not an expert on how vampires are made. I've never made one. But I do know that newly made vampires don't just spontaneously resurrect. Their maker needs to be present for that to happen. In this case, Hunt coming to the morgue triggered the awakening."

I stared at him aghast. "But that would mean…"

He nodded. "That Miss Peaches was made into a vampire by Morgan Hunt."

"But why?" I couldn't fathom it. "Finch would make sense, but Hunt?"

"Because he can?" Amber suggested. Luca nodded.

"It's not like there's thousands of us, so whenever a vampire runs across someone who can be turned, they usually do—if they know how."

"Then why didn't he tell us?"

Third Spell's the Charm

"Maybe he didn't want to get your hopes up," Giselle said.

"Maybe he forgot," Luca countered dryly. "Old vampires sometimes get like that."

I wasn't exactly an expert on Hunt, but I shook my head. "He seems like a man who never forgets anything, ever."

Luca gave me a wry look in agreement.

"So Hunt is the killer after all?" Giselle asked, but Luca shook his head.

"Not necessarily, if he reached her soon enough after her death."

I tried to imagine Hunt leaning over Miss Peaches in the cramped booth of the club to do whatever was needed to make a vampire, and my mind balked.

"I'm not happy that Danielle is back in town," Amber said after she'd taken a moment to digest our story. "And now the warlock is here too."

I remembered the ease with which Dufort went about her house. "I don't think she ever truly left."

Amber made a face.

"What do you think has happened to her?" Giselle asked, concerned.

I spread my arms. "Impossible to tell. But I think it's safe to say she's with Finch voluntarily."

"Why would you say that?"

"The tracing Kane and Dufort did clearly indicated she was at Finch's house after the fire, and then she was gone. I'd say that means she can go about freely."

"Then why hasn't she come home?" Luca asked.

"Maybe she and Dufort have broken up again, but he didn't want to tell us."

"In which case we're helping him to fetch back a woman who might not want to be with him." He didn't look happy about the idea. Can't say I was either.

"Maybe she returns home by morning and we don't have to care about their relationship drama."

"She's the only one who knows what's going on," he reminded me.

"Then let's hope she's willing to share." I yawned and almost dislocated my jaw. "Sorry."

Giselle smiled. "I think we'll call it a night. It's been eventful as is."

Exhausted beyond words, I dragged myself to bed. I feared the events of the night would keep me awake, but I underestimated Giselle's tea. I'd barely crawled into bed when I was already asleep and only woke up when Ashley banged at my door.

"If you don't shut off that alarm right now, I'll come in there and do it for you. Permanently."

Sixteen

I FUMBLED AT MY ALARM BLINDLY and managed to switch it off, then forced my eyes open before I fell asleep again. According to the alarm clock, I'd slept ten minutes with the alarm beeping. No wonder Ashley was annoyed.

I entered the kitchen half an hour later, mostly awake. But apparently I'd dressed up asleep, because I had no recollection of choosing a blue sheath dress that I'd meant to save for the auction, and my hair was in a chignon instead of a ponytail. At least I'd donned the leather jacket and boots again, so I didn't look quite so ladies-who-lunch.

Ashley was polishing off a plate of full English breakfast, heavy on bacon and sausages, but she paused to glare at me. "How can anyone sleep that long with such annoying beeping?"

I sat across from her, and Giselle gave me tea and fruit. I'd had to give up bacon and eggs, and pretty much everything delicious she cooked. My spin classes and running simply couldn't keep up.

"I think Giselle overdid her soothing tea last night."

Giselle grimaced. "I'm sorry. You were so spooked and exhausted from that spell that I gave you extra."

"Oh, I needed it. Lucky thing Ashley has good ears and a short temper, or I'd still be asleep."

Luca ambled into the kitchen. He never showed up at breakfast, as he was usually fast asleep. He went to the stove and Giselle filled a plate for him.

Ashley shot him a sharp look after he'd sat down. "Were you at my fire site yesterday?"

He looked puzzled. "Didn't Ronnie tell you?"

"I meant after it was cooled."

He sniffed at his clothes even though he'd changed since yesterday, but maybe he hadn't washed his hair. "Is it the smell? Can you tell fires apart based on it?"

"No," she huffed, then reconsidered. "Well, yes, but it's more that there was only one housefire yesterday and the bitter smell of burning wood doused with water is unmistakeable, the way it sticks to you."

That's werewolves for you.

"Yes, we went in last night," I told her while Luca was inhaling his food. "We were looking for Danielle. She's missing."

She straightened. "Was the body hers?"

"Not according to her warlock boyfriend."

"Dufort's here too?" She sighed. "He's dreamy. Evil, but dreamy."

I had to agree.

"Whose is the body, then? The owner?"

"Not according to Hunt, at least not officially. The owner is a vampire, so he was likely faking his death with this."

Third Spell's the Charm

Her mouth pressed in a line of displeasure. "Fires aren't something you play with. Did you figure out how it started?"

"No, but we know how it was contained. Danielle warded the place."

Her brows shot up. "That's something at least. Dad will have to control this carefully or there's going to be one very confused fire inspector trying to figure this out."

"I can give the inspector false memories," Luca promised, and she nodded gratefully.

"I'll let you know if it's needed."

Luca pushed his empty plate away and leaned back in his chair, crossing arms over his chest. "Do you think we should try to find Danielle today?"

"Maybe she's come home already?" I suggested hopefully.

"Ronnie would've told us."

Ashley frowned. "You mixed my baby brother up into this?"

"Hunt kind of did," Luca said defensively. "But he volunteered to watch Danielle's house for her return."

I sighed. "I have no idea where to even start to look for her."

"I think it's safe to assume that she's with Finch. Maybe we should concentrate on him instead."

"Good idea. Not that he'll be any easier to find. He's planned this for a long time, all the deaths and the fire. He likely has a good hiding place." I lifted my teacup, but put it back down when a question occurred to me.

"Why would Finch kill Miss Peaches? It would've made sense if he was the one who made her a vampire, but this..."

"Miss Peaches is a vampire now?" Ashley exclaimed, horrified. "Poor thing."

"Hey, it's not such a bad life," Luca protested, then grimaced. "But it does take a while to get used to. Maybe Finch didn't want this kind of existence for her."

"But why kill her, then?"

He ran a hand through his already messy hair. "Maybe she surprised him in the act and had to be silenced? Or maybe it was anger for the breakup?"

I nodded, my mind racing. "Maybe she was the real target all along, and the others were killed to divert our attention away from him."

"Then why did he kidnap Shepard?"

That made me pause. "Jealousy? Maybe he and Miss Peaches were having an affair and that was the real reason for her breakup with Finch."

"That makes as much sense as anything," he said. "Now we only have to figure out how Danielle fits into this and why Finch went after Hunt."

"Easy…"

He grinned. "We have the surveillance footage. The software should start giving out results today."

I rose from the table. "Let me know if anything interesting pops up. I'll research Finch. Do you remember the name he used after Vaughn?"

He frowned. "Carl Davis, if I recall. But it could've been a later name too."

"It's better than nothing."

I'D STAYED SO LONG at breakfast that I had to hurry to work, no time to pause for scenery. I cut through the park by the Charterhouse, always a pleasant option that saved me a few minutes on my walk to Barbican Station. So it

Third Spell's the Charm

wasn't until I was exiting Bond Street Station to Oxford Street that I saw the tabloid headlines:
Mysterious Deaths At Nightclubs!

I stopped so abruptly that the person hurrying out after me almost collided with me. He apologised as he rounded me and I said, "Not at all," as if it hadn't been my fault.

I was sitting at my desk reading the article when Kane arrived. "Ah, you saw it too," he said.

"This is worse than the first. There's nothing substantial, but enough insinuation that the average reader will think Hunt killed those people."

He shook his head. "Finch had a busy day yesterday: a kidnap and a housefire, and now this."

I made a face, then gave him a hesitant look. "Have you heard anything about Danielle?"

His jaw tightened. "No. You'd best figure out where Finch could be hiding."

Since I'd planned to do just that, I set out to search for him the moment Kane disappeared into his office.

It was easy enough to trace him from George Vaughn to Carl Davis to three other identities before reaching Finch. Everything was nicely documented and digitised, wills and property listings alike. He'd steadily built a substantial real-estate portfolio, the bulk of it in London.

Provided that he'd listed everything truthfully—which wasn't at all certain—there were no abandoned warehouses or factories that would make an excellent hideout. I'd have to go through every house he owned one by one to see if they would make a good lair. Thank goodness for Google maps.

Luca called midmorning. "The facial recognition software has begun to give out results, and they're not what we expected."

"Oh?"

"It's mostly security guards who apparently rotate between clubs."

Blast.

"What about Finch?"

"He isn't in any of the footage so far."

"That's vexing. Surely he is our killer?" I hadn't even considered he wouldn't be, after what had happened the previous day. "Could one of the security be a vampire?"

He made a dubious noise. "With so many werewolves there? I don't think so. But I'll ask Ronnie. And let's not be discouraged yet. There are results still to come."

Kane emerged from his office after I'd finished the call. "How is it going?"

"Not well. There are too many options. And according to Luca, Finch doesn't appear in the CCTV footage."

He glanced at his wristwatch. "I think we'd best review our options over lunch."

He didn't often invite me, so I got up eagerly. "Do you have a particular place in mind?"

He nodded. "Hunt invited us to lunch at the club we both belong to."

Good thing I'd worn decent clothes today.

We took a taxi to St James' Street. The club was for businesspeople, and allowed women as members too, unlike the so called "traditional" gentlemen's clubs. It was located across the road from Boodles, a gentlemen's club that was a year younger than Hunt—or Armand de Morganville—and closer to the Piccadilly end of the street

Third Spell's the Charm

than St James's Palace. The yellow-brick neoclassical building wasn't the largest there, only three stories with square white half-columns running all the way to the pediment, but it was elegant and well-maintained.

The entrance was straight from the pavement in an unostentatious recess, and there was no plaque on the wall or the door announcing what was there. You had to know the club existed to find it.

Inside, an elegant foyer continued the same neoclassical style. There was a reception desk at one side. A man in livery greeted Kane with a smile.

"Mr Kane, so good to see you after such a long time."

Kane nodded at him in greeting. "I've been unfortunately busy lately, Pitts. I'm here to lunch with Mr Hunt. I brought a guest."

Pitts nodded at me and smiled in approval. I wondered what the reception would've been if I'd worn jeans. Maybe my subconscious had known this would happen today and had chosen the dress accordingly.

Pitts gave us a visitors' log to sign. "Mr Hunt isn't here yet. Would you like to wait in the salon?"

"Thank you."

Kane led me to a room on the right of the hall, an airy space with dove grey walls and white panel mouldings. The furniture continued the neoclassical theme and was more decorative than comfortable. There were several seating groups and single chairs, and only a couple of the latter were occupied, by elderly gentlemen.

Retirees were probably the only kinds of businessmen who had time to hang out at a club these days.

We chose a late Louis XV style seating group with dark grey velvet upholstering in a white wooden frame. They were in such good repair that I would've said they were modern, but Kane informed me that they were from the 1940s and were by *Maison Jansen*, a French furniture maker of great renown.

"I acquired these myself."

He looked pleased with himself, and I agreed. Older *Maison Jansen* furniture were difficult to come by, and they were expensive. A pair of chairs much like the one I was sitting on had recently sold for five thousand pounds.

They weren't terribly comfortable chairs, considering this was a salon for members to spend time in, but I was so tense that I wouldn't have been comfortable in a feather bed.

A waiter showed up with a small glass of port for Kane and a sherry for me. Apparently drinks were gendered even in a club that allowed women as members. I wanted to drain the whole glass to ease my nerves, but I didn't dare to. With Hunt, I'd need all my wits. I took a small sip, only to almost choke on it when a male voice addressed me.

"Phoebe?"

I PLACED THE GLASS carefully on the table in front of me and rose to greet my uncle.

John Radcliff wasn't really my uncle but the husband of my cousin, Emilia, daughter of my Aunt Clara, father's sister. The age difference between Emilia and me was such that I'd always regarded her as my aunt. Their daughter, Olivia, was my age.

Ever since my father retired from the family business after a heart attack and moved to France with Mother, Uncle John had run the company. He was a nice, unassuming man in his fifties, and I liked him very much.

Third Spell's the Charm

"What brings you here?" he asked, leaning down for a brief hug.

"I'm here with my boss." I gestured at Kane, introducing the men. Kane rose to shake hands with him.

"Has the young couple returned from their honeymoon yet?" I then asked.

Olivia had married a couple of weeks ago after a whirlwind romance. The wedding had almost been cancelled because of Jack, the bastard of a mage, who'd wanted to put pressure on me by ruining it, but everything worked out in the end.

He smiled warmly. "They returned on Sunday. You should come over for a dinner to see them. Would Saturday suit you?"

"I'm afraid we have a huge auction then." I had true regret in my voice. I wasn't terribly close with Olivia, but we'd sort of bonded over the trouble Jack had caused.

"Next week, then?"

I smiled. "That would be better."

The waiter returned, interrupting us. "Mr Hunt has arrived."

My uncle's brows shot up. "Moving up in the world?"

"He's my boss's acquaintance."

I couldn't very well tell him I was investigating deaths by vampire for Hunt, who was a perfectly normal businessman as far as my uncle was concerned.

"Well, it never hurts to make connections," he said, sounding so like Aunt Clara that I grinned. He smiled too, indicating he had used the tone his mother-in-law often applied on purpose.

I was more relaxed when I followed Kane and the waiter to the large, airy dining room at the other end of the floor. It was full of businesspeople of all ages, genders, and nationalities, and I even recognised a few faces from newspapers and magazines. The waiter led us across the room to a small cabinet at the back, and closed the door behind us with a discreet click.

Hunt was waiting at the head of the table. And he wasn't alone.

My stomach sank. Dufort. Wearing a suit easily as expensive as Hunt's. I wondered fleetingly if he'd portaled to France to get it. The dark grey business suit, with a light pink shirt of all colours, fit him perfectly—and didn't make him look any less scary.

The vampire and the warlock rose with old world politeness and actually bowed. I don't know if they even realised they were doing it. Kane nodded back with similar grace, but I refused to curtsy, no matter how old the men with me were. But bowing didn't come naturally to me either, and I stood there stiff and awkward.

Hunt gestured for us to take seats and we complied, sitting across the table from Dufort. I let Kane take the chair closest to Hunt.

"I took the liberty of ordering for all of us," Hunt said affably, as if this was a perfectly normal social situation. "I hope salmon is fine with everyone."

The waiter returned just then, pushing in a serving trolley laden with our dishes. He delivered them swiftly, poured us wine, and left as discreetly as he had entered.

The food on the plate looked delicious and the scent was even better, but I was tense again and the mere notion of eating made me nauseous. The men didn't have the same problem. They picked up their utensils and dug in—elegantly.

Third Spell's the Charm

"I think it's best we recap everything that's happened so far," Hunt said, reaching for his glass. "Maybe Phoebe could sum things up."

There went what little appetite I had.

"And make it as thorough as possible for those who are only now joining in," Dufort added, looking like he was truly interested in our detective game.

I took a sip of my wine, both for encouragement and to play for time. But there was no getting over the fact that I'd have to tell Hunt about the research on him I'd done.

I gave Dufort a quick recap about the bodies left in Hunt's clubs. When I was done, he nodded. "I saw the headlines. I didn't realise it was about you."

Hunt's brows furrowed. "I had nothing to do with the deaths like the rag insinuates. I may have to take legal action against them this time."

"Is it the same journalist?" Kane asked and Hunt nodded. "Maybe we should talk to them?"

"If the vampire has scrambled his head, it's no use."

"Maybe the vampire is the journalist," Kane countered.

I managed to eat a few bites while they argued about the merits of talking to the journalist. They decided to let be for now. Then it was time for me to fess up.

Seventeen

I GLANCED AT HUNT, BUT ADDRESSED Dufort. "I've been searching Mr Hunt's past for an enemy who might be behind this."

"I told you to leave be," Hunt growled, but Dufort looked intrigued.

"How far in his past did you get?"

"To 1761."

Dufort nodded, impressed. Hunt was staring at me with his mouth open.

"How did you manage that?"

Since he wasn't immediately going to explode, I told the truth: "I was curious about the book you were so eager to purchase from us, *The Fantastical Creatures of British Islands*. It had a portrait of you as Armand de Morganville."

"How did you find a copy?"

I shrugged, as if it hadn't been difficult. "There's a digital version on the *18th Century Books Online*."

His power rose, fast and fierce, making the glasses chime and pulling the air from the room. Kane made a quick gesture, shielding me from it. I was grateful, but I decided then and there to learn to do it myself.

Well, obviously only after I'd stopped setting everything on fire with my spells.

The power cut off as abruptly as it had risen, and gathering himself, Hunt gestured for me to continue. I cleared my throat.

"I traced you to 1898, when you worked with George Vaughn, who later becomes Adam Finch, the vampire whose house Danielle warded and later burned." The latter was for Dufort's benefit. "As far as we know, he's the vampire after Hunt."

Hunt shook his head. "I've told you a hundred times: nothing happened between Vaughn and me to merit waiting for revenge for a hundred and twenty years."

"Maybe you disparaged his work, or ruined his reputation?" I suggested. "Because that's what he's trying to do to you now."

"And you've changed identities so often that it's possible he only now realised who Morgan Hunt is," Kane added.

"I haven't left London for a century. He would've known who I am."

That did put a crimp in our theory. "But Finch is involved somehow."

Kane pursed his lips. "Or maybe he got involved only after his ex was killed."

He had a point.

"What about Maxim Shepard, then?" Hunt asked. "How does he fit in to this?"

I gestured with my wine glass I'd been about to sip. "Luca and I think it might be jealousy. Miss Peaches worked for Shepard, so maybe they were having an affair. Maybe Finch went after him as revenge."

"So the kidnapping has nothing to do with me?"

Third Spell's the Charm

"Likely so." I put the glass down without drinking and tried to resume eating. "If you're right about Finch faking his death with the fire, maybe he wanted to tie up loose ends before he moves elsewhere."

Hunt cocked a brow. "So the body belongs to Shephard?"

My stomach tightened uncomfortably, but since we had no way of knowing, I left the matter be and continued.

"There is one thing speaking against Finch as the killer. Luca has had first results from the facial recognition software, and according to him the only people repeatedly at all your clubs are the security. Finch isn't in any of the footage."

"I told you!" Hunt looked vindicated.

"But if it's not him, we have absolutely no idea who the enemy is. Do you employ vampires as security? Maybe it's one of them. They would certainly have the opportunity."

Hunt's face tightened. "I have a couple, but neither of them is strong enough to hide what they are."

"That you know of," Kane said, but Hunt shook his head.

"I'm responsible for turning them. They're babies."

It was as good an opening as I was going to get. "Why did you turn Miss Peaches?"

He shrugged. "Partly because she was a potential candidate and I hate for those to go to waste. I reached her soon enough after her death that it could be done. But mostly it's because I'm hoping she can tell me who killed her."

I stared at him. "That didn't even occur to me. What did she say?"

"If I knew the killer we wouldn't be here," he said dryly. "She hasn't recovered well enough to speak yet. Or *he*, as I was informed he's Sam now and not Miss Peaches after the costume came off."

I tried to wrap my mind around it, after thinking of her—him—as Miss Peaches the whole time.

"Could I see him, maybe jolt his memory?"

He made a slashing motion with his hand. "Absolutely not. Newly made vampires are too volatile and dangerous, in constant need of blood. You'd end up as his snack and most likely die. They cannot stop feeding."

"So … he now kills?"

The idea of the cheerful person I'd met killing in ravenous rage made my stomach churn.

"Give me a little credit. I obviously feed him with bottled blood."

"Is that possible?" I asked, amazed, and he pulled back.

"Why wouldn't it be?"

I made a vague gesture with my fork. "It never is in stories."

"Is this about *Buffy* again?" he asked in a fed-up voice.

I couldn't recall if it had ever come up in it. "All of them. It's accepted as canon."

He leaned his elbows on the table and steepled his hands under his chin, looking at me like he was addressing a child. "That was before blood could be stored outside a human body. When I was young, no one even considered the possibility of extracting blood into bottles. Transfusions weren't a thing and there weren't any refrigerators or freezers to keep it fresh. Now there are. And it's perfectly suitable for our purposes."

It made sense, put like that.

"And when he recovers? What if the killer isn't anyone he recognises?"

"So you agree it's not Finch?"

An annoyed huff escaped my mouth for his stubbornness. "He's involved somehow, but I was thinking of your security. No one ever pays attention to them. If it's not any of the vampires you've made, it could be someone you believe to be a human."

He furrowed his brows, then nodded. "I have to investigate."

Dufort looked grim. "Even if this Finch vampire isn't the one who is attacking you, he still has Danielle."

I nodded. "He commissioned her to ward his house. But why she chose to help him with the rest, I have no idea."

"Helping a vampire?" Dufort's voice was full of contempt. Hunt looked at him down his nose.

"If you want my assistance in finding her, you keep those comments to yourself."

I continued hastily: "Whatever her role, she's done more than the wards and driving the car, because Luca said non-vampire magic was used in Shepard's office when he was kidnapped. Finch could've simply mesmerised Shepard and she wasn't there in person, so it had to be Finch casting the spell—unless Shepard is a mage. But could Finch have overpowered him in that case?"

Kane frowned. "I can't recall a mage called Shepard in London. And I'm not aware of any way to give another person the ability to cast spells."

Dufort sneered. "It can be done."

Kane shot him a sharp look. "Care to clarify that?"

"No."

Meaning it had to be a warlock skill. Which meant Danielle had to be further into her transformation into an evil, murderous being.

Wonderful.

"Whether or not she's doing it voluntarily, the fact remains that she and Finch need to be found."

Hunt turned to Dufort. "Could you try another tracing spell?"

Dufort shook his head. "I already tried, and it didn't bring results. She can't be found."

Silence fell. No one wanted to suggest that it might mean she was dead.

"Could she be hidden behind a shield of some kind that blocks magic?" I asked Kane. He frowned, thinking.

"Technically, yes. But she's the only mage in their group, and if she's not there voluntarily, why would she hide herself?"

"So maybe she is there voluntarily."

"And not tell me?" Dufort asked, incredulous. I chose not to remind him that she had fled him once, and instead turned to Hunt.

"Could a vampire create such a shield?"

He shook his head. "We can't create wards or shields with our kind of magic."

"At all?"

"I could trace the figures all night long. They wouldn't do anything."

"No mage has ever been turned to a vampire?" I quipped, but to my bafflement, he stiffened. His eyes narrowed.

"I have heard tales. But such vampires would be extremely rare. I would know if Finch was one."

Third Spell's the Charm

Kane tapped fingers against the table, like was his habit when he wrestled with a problem. "I'm not familiar with any tracking spells that could see through wards meant to hide a person. Do you?" he asked Dufort, who shook his head. Kane straightened.

"I think it's time we talk with Rupert."

"Who's Rupert?" Dufort demanded.

"The archmage of London." Kane sneered. "And he doesn't like Danielle. So you'd best hope he's in a good mood."

IF THERE'S ONE THING that wasn't done, it was bringing a warlock and a vampire to meet an archmage—especially this one. So we parted ways after lunch. Hunt had mundane business meetings to handle, and Dufort returned to Danielle's home in case she showed up.

Rupert Barnet, the archmage of London—there could be only one—lived in a brown brick Victorian villa in Highbury Crescent, about five miles northeast from the club. It had a small front garden, which had been overgrown when I visited here last. Now it was nicely trimmed, matching the garden of the other half of the two-family house.

"I contracted a landscaping firm," Kane told me, then flashed a smile: "Paid for it too. It's useless to expect Rupert to part with a single penny he doesn't want to."

The previous time, it had taken forever for Rupert's ancient butler, Jones, to answer the door. Now it was opened in no time, and the reason for the speed was obvious: it wasn't Jones. We were greeted by a sturdy woman in her fifties in a sensible light green uniform of loose trousers and short-sleeved top, much like those worn by nurses or cleaners.

"Good afternoon, Mrs Turner. Is Rupert in?"

"Afternoon, Mr Kane. He's always in. Whether he will he see you is another matter." She stepped aside and we filed in. "But he's always in a better mood after you've visited, so go ahead and go in. He's in the parlour."

"This is my assistant, Miss Thorpe," Kane introduced me, and I nodded at the woman. "Mrs Turner is the housekeeper we insisted Rupert hire."

"And none too soon, if you ask me, the way the house was," Mrs Turner said with a longsuffering sigh. Jones was frail and almost deaf, and hadn't really been able to manage anything but the barest minimum.

"Not that Jones will admit it. And can I make him rest?" She shook her head as Jones tottered across the hall just then, peering at us through his rheumy eyes.

"I have this handled," Mrs Turner said in a louder voice to him. "Let's return to the kitchen." She wrapped an arm around Jones', turning him around.

"Good to see you, sir," Jones greeted Kane when we went past.

"You too, Jones."

I followed Kane down the hallway to a room towards the back garden, noticing as I went that the house had been thoroughly cleaned since my last visit. Mrs Turner was clearly an efficient housekeeper. Light reached in through the windows now that the grime was gone and curtains were open, and there wasn't a speck of dust anywhere.

Kane knocked on the door at the end of the hallway. "Go away!" a man shouted inside, but Kane ignored it and opened the door.

"Oh, it's you," Rupert said, sounding grumpy. "What do you want? We're not due to another lesson, are we?"

Third Spell's the Charm

We entered the room that was full of Victorian furniture, much like the living room at the House of Magic, but more faded. Only one tasselled floor lamp had been switched on, offering light for the occupant of a tall wingback chair. Last time I'd visited, the chair had been by the window, but now it was by a gas fireplace opposite the door. The fire had been lit too.

Like previously, Rupert was dressed in a faded red smoking jacket and grey flannel trousers. According to Kane, he was close to a hundred, if not older—archmages could live long lives—but there was only a small bit of grey in his thick, auburn hair, and the wrinkles on his face were mostly around his sharp eyes. I'd witnessed him handle a warlock-in-making without tiring, casting spells that would've brought a younger man to his knees.

"Good afternoon, Rupert. No, I'm not here for a lesson. I need help with locating a person."

Rupert gave Kane a pointed look. "What's wrong with your skills that you can't perform a basic tracing?"

"We believe she's been hidden behind a protective ward of some sort."

"I was hidden behind such a thing and it didn't stop you from finding me," Rupert pointed out. He had been taken captive by said warlock-in-making, Julius Blackhart, but Kane had spelled a pen to act as a tracker that pulled us to the correct place.

"Yet we're unable to do it this time."

"Maybe she's dead," Rupert stated mercilessly. Kane's jaw tightened, but he nodded.

"It's possible."

"So who's missing?"

"Danielle."

Rupert glowered. "That woman? Why would I help

you find her? She's nothing but trouble. You're better off without her."

"I'm not looking for her for myself," Kane said patiently, but Rupert gave him a slow look, clearly not believing him.

"Then why do it at all?"

"Because it's the decent thing to do? She's been taken captive by a vampire, and her ... partner ... misses her."

"The warlock?" Rupert asked sharply. Kane's brows rose.

"You've heard of him?"

"Just because I spend most of my time here doesn't mean I don't get the news," he said smugly. "So why don't the warlock trace her?"

"He's been unable to do it either."

"Hmmm..." He turned his attention to me, brows furrowing. "And why are you here?"

"We could use your help with her too," Kane answered smoothly for me.

"Again?" He glowered at me from under his brows. "What have you done this time?"

The previous time that we'd needed his help had been for the spell Jack had put on me, which hadn't been my fault, but I decided it was best not to bring that up.

"It's more about what I can't do," I sighed.

"Phoebe has been learning to cast spells, but inexplicably, every spell ends in something catching fire."

I gave Rupert a gloomy nod. "Usually my hair."

Rupert stared at us for a heartbeat. Then he threw his head back and cackled a laugh. "I grant you this, boy, you truly liven my days."

Kane took this in a stride. "Have you come across this sort of problem before?"

"I can't say I have, but that doesn't mean no one has. Let's see, then. Cast a spell."

He gestured at me to come to him, but I hesitated. "Maybe inside a protective circle?"

"Nonsense. How bad can it be?"

"Bad," Kane and I said in unison.

Rupert gave a longsuffering sigh and pushed himself up from the chair. "We'd better go upstairs, then."

His gait was brisk as we followed him out of the parlour to the stairs in the entrance hall. "We'll be in my study and not to be bothered," he said to Mrs Turner, who was coming down.

"But what about tea?"

"Hang your tea, woman."

Mrs Turner rolled her eyes but didn't say anything as we passed her on our way to the top floor. Rupert was slightly winded when we reached there, but no more than I, and he didn't slow down as he headed down the hall to a large empty room he used for his spellcasting.

It wasn't truly empty. The contents had been hidden with magic.

"I'd best put a ward on the door, just in case that woman thinks to bring us tea after all," Rupert grumped, waving his hand at the lock in what to my inexpert eyes looked like too vague a gesture to be a proper ward or spell, but the tingling on my skin indicated that magic was being used.

"You really should've gotten me a housekeeper who knows about magic."

Kane nodded. "Those weren't readily available."

"Hmph." Rupert gestured with his hand again, at Kane this time. "Well, go ahead, draw a protective circle for the girl."

205

Kane did as commanded, drawing the same complicated circles as when we'd practiced at the shop, but only for me this time. Rupert studied them with a frown.

"That's going to prevent the spell from taking."

"Only inside the circle where she'll be. It'll take in that smaller circle."

When the circles were done, Kane gestured for me to step into the larger one. He and Rupert weren't protected, but they could shield if needed.

"Which spells do you know?" Rupert asked.

"Water and wind."

"Let's see, then."

I found it amazingly difficult to concentrate with the archmage watching. Gritting my teeth, I managed to reach into the spark inside me and form the correct gestures while saying the spell aloud. No water appeared in the smaller circle, but nothing caught fire either.

"That was disappointing," Rupert said. My shoulders slumped, but Kane simply fetched a piece of paper and placed it in the smaller circle. He gave me an encouraging smile.

"Try again."

This time the paper caught fire.

Rupert stared at it with his brows raised. "Huh. Try the wind now."

Kane placed a feather in the smaller circle, and I cast the correct spell—with the incorrect results.

Rupert cackled. "That is bizarre. Can you do the fire spell?"

"Not intentionally," I said dryly, and he cackled again.

"Let me show you."

Eighteen

I HESITATED. "Is it wise?"

He waved his arms impatiently. "Of course it's wise. That way you'll know the difference between a true and accidental fire spell." He noticed my doubt and glared. "What would you like to learn, then?"

"I was thinking of a protective shield…"

Kane nodded, approving, but Rupert frowned. "What for?"

"To defend myself?"

"A girl like you shouldn't need such a spell."

"You'd be surprised," I said dryly, and he relented.

"Fine. It's not much more complicated, and there's a shortcut that you'll learn once you've mastered the long form."

I nodded. "I don't have trouble with memorising the gestures and incantations, it's only the result that's wrong."

"Good. This basic shield is a variation of the wind spell."

My stomach fell. "Wonderful…"

He ignored my comment. "Instead of moving the air, you're solidifying it. Imagine an actual shield as you cast the spell, any shape or size, but the thicker the air wall you can create, the better it blocks simple spells."

"But only simple ones," Kane added. "If you want to shield against offensive spells like those in magic battles, you need better shields."

"Does this shield against Hunt's power?"

"Hunt? The vampire?" Rupert asked, outraged. "What do you have to do with him?"

"It's complicated," Kane said. "But we're currently trying to solve a problem that might affect the entire magical community if it becomes public."

Rupert harrumphed but let it be. "Here are the gestures," he told me, showing them clearly and with fingers more agile than people his age usually had.

They were similar to the wind spell, only backwards, so it took a moment for me to twist my mind accordingly. When I'd mastered the gestures, he taught me the incantation. It was slightly more complicated than in the wind spell, but not impossible to learn or remember.

"Now, step out of the circle."

"What?"

He gave me a pointed look. "How are we to test whether the shields work if you're already inside a protective circle?"

That did make sense, but I was reluctant. "I could set the whole room on fire."

"We'll take that risk."

I wasn't quite as willing to risk my hair, but I did as I was told. Like with all spells, I concentrated, found the spark and coaxed it out, then cast the spell slowly and carefully, imagining a shield as wide and tall as I was, a bit difficult as I couldn't see it.

Third Spell's the Charm

The felt the spell take, so I had to be casting it correctly, and to my amazement nothing started to burn. "Did it work?"

"Let's see," Rupert said, and threw a spell at me.

Small fires burst in the air in front of me when it hit my shield, startling me to break my concentration. The shield disappeared.

"What happened?" I asked, my heart beating too fast. Rupert tilted his head, and Kane looked intrigued.

"Fascinating..." Rupert muttered. "Let's try again."

I had to recast the shield, but it came easier this time. It was as if I could sense the shield in front of me now. When it was ready, Rupert attacked me again and fires hit the shield again. I was more prepared, but the bursts right in front of my face were unnerving and the shield broke.

Rupert stroked his chin. "Well, the good news is your shield works. The bad news is that whatever is wrong with your spellcasting affects this too."

"Does it feel different?" Kane asked. I gave him a baffled look.

"Different how?"

"From the other two spells?"

I tilted my head. "No...?"

"It didn't drain more energy?" he confirmed, and I shook my head.

"I ... can't really tell, after spending so much energy already."

"Hmmm..."

Rupert took a piece of chalk from the pocket of his smoking jacket, and surprisingly agilely, leaned down to draw new circles on the floor, different from Kane's. My boss kept a keen eye on what he drew, nodding.

This time Rupert went inside the smaller circle, indicating I should take the larger one. "The water spell first, please."

I stared at him horrified. "I'll burn you."

"No you won't. The spell won't take in the circles I've drawn, but it'll allow me to sense them."

Still anxious, I obeyed. To my immense relief, Rupert didn't burst to fire, but he just nodded.

"The wind spell next."

I cast it, and then the shield. Nothing burned, but Rupert didn't look satisfied.

"Each spell you cast felt exactly the same," he said, getting out of the circle.

"And that's bad?"

He gestured with his hand, irritated. "Of course it's bad. But it's also good, because now we can get to the root of your problem."

"A conduit issue?" Kane suggested.

"Or a block. Or both."

They launched into a conversation about the causes and remedies of whatever was wrong with my spellcasting—or me. The problem engrossing them, they moved to Rupert's study without a word to me.

I stared after them for a moment. Then, sighing, I exited the circle, fetched a mop, and cleaned the chalk off the floor.

They hadn't reached an agreement by the time I followed them to the study. They'd pulled out a pile of books and opened them on every available surface—which there weren't many—and were both deep into reading. I could only hope they were the ones containing explanations or cures for me, and not some other interesting tomes they had happened to spot. Neither of

Third Spell's the Charm

them was paying any attention to me or each other, only muttering to themselves, annoyed or excited, as they turned the pages impatiently.

The books were visible for a change; the shelves had been spelled to look empty the last time I was here. Infinitely curious, I began to read the backs of the books that filled the wall-to-wall shelves.

As could be expected, there were spell books from all ages and in many different languages. Some of them were printed, but many were manuscripts bound in leather, with faded gilt lettering on the spines. There were books on astronomy and astrology, books on gems and alchemy, potion making books, and books on magical items.

I didn't touch any of them, but my fingers itched with the last one. Maybe it contained pictures of cursed statuettes for me to avoid in the future.

That made me remember the original reason we came here for. "What about Danielle?"

The men paused, giving me distracted and baffled looks. "Sorry?" Kane said, and I barely refrained from rolling my eyes.

"Danielle? Your ex-wife who's currently held captive by a vampire?"

"Right…" Reluctantly, he put the book he was reading away and looked at Rupert.

"Is there anything that would help us reach through the shield?"

Rupert didn't look any happier about helping Danielle than before, but he nodded, impatiently. "What are you using as a focus?"

Kane pulled out the vial of Danielle's blood from his pocket and showed it to Rupert. My brows shot up. The archmage's hair began to billow in anger and rising magic, much like Kane's.

"Why do you have that thing?" he bellowed. Kane was unfazed by his fury.

"The warlock, Laurent Dufort, gave it to me."

"Of course he did..." Rupert's magic eased, but his foul mood remained. "Well, it should do fine. We need to amplify it before you try the trace. Give it a boost as a focus."

Kane nodded, his face clearing in understanding. "Of course. Why didn't I come to think of that..."

"Why indeed?" Rupert said, dryly. "It's a two-mage spell. I'll help you with it and then you can go elsewhere for the tracking spell, and I can continue my research."

The men returned to the workroom. I made to follow, interested in this new spell, but a wave of exhaustion washed over me. My eyesight blackened and I had to lean heavily against Rupert's writing desk. I'd never done so many spells in a row and the strain had caught up with me.

Rupert and Kane didn't need me watching over them. Moreover, I wasn't in a proper frame of mind to learn anything by observing them.

Instead, I continued my browsing of the shelves. One section had biographies, journals, and other books of and by mages themselves, a veritable who's who in magicdom. To my amazement, I spotted a familiar name: Bernard Bishop, the author of the book Hunt had purchased from us. It was a biography written by Charles Bishop, though it wasn't immediately obvious what their relations had been.

Had Bishop been a mage and not an ordinary scholar? Then why had he had the facts about vampires so wrong?

Third Spell's the Charm

Curious, I pulled the book out and opened it. On the front page was a picture of Bishop himself, a lithograph reproduction of an oil portrait painted in his later years. A fairly unremarkable looking man in a full Georgian wig and the simpler attire of a country gentleman. I studied the picture carefully, but he wasn't anyone I recognised from the present day.

Since the men were still occupied with the spell, I began to read the book. The early years were a boring exultation of Bishop by Charles, who turned out to be his son, but he hadn't been a mage, so I wasn't sure why the book was on Rupert's shelf. After a while, I started to skim the chapters for interesting details. I found one towards the end of the book.

It turned out that publishing *The Fantastical Creatures* had gained Bishop public ridicule and the scorn of his peers, academic and social alike. Incensed, he'd spent the years after its publication writing treatises and letters arguing his book was based on research and true facts. The end part of Charles's book was dedicated to this.

Among the points of contention was the identity of Armand de Morganville who, curiously, wasn't himself arguing with Bishop, leaving it to his peers, though according to Charles, he was egging them on. I recognised some of the names from history books, one of them a future prime minister, but there were no pictures of those I didn't recognise, and I couldn't tell if they were anyone I should pay attention to in case they turned out to be vampires operating in London today.

I found the book fascinating. When the men returned to the study, having finished their spell, I showed it to Rupert. "May I borrow this?"

His brows furrowed. "What is it?"

"A biography of an eighteenth century scholar named Bernard Bishop."

"What do you need that for?"

"I'm currently researching him."

He pulled back. "Why?"

"Morgan Hunt was interested in him. And he seemed to hate Hunt."

His gaze sharpened. "Is that so? In that case, take the book. But no underlining."

I promised to cherish it.

"What about Phoebe's problem?" Kane asked, and Rupert made an impatient wave with his hand.

"I'll figure something out. You can leave now."

Kane and I exchanged amused glances, but thanked Rupert and fled the study before he could change his mind about the book.

It might be nothing, but a tingle in my spine told me it was important.

LUCA WAS MANNING the shop while Amber was handling bookkeeping, but she abandoned them eagerly when Kane asked her help with the tracing spell. She instantly headed upstairs to inform Giselle and start to prepare for the spell. Kane followed her, but I asked to be left out. The mere thought of climbing to the attic exhausted me.

"Did you learn anything?" Luca asked, abandoning his laptop he'd been studying.

I showed him the book. "I'm reading about Hunt's feud with Bernard Bishop in the eighteenth century."

He looked intrigued. "Do you think he's the vampire causing this?"

Third Spell's the Charm

I showed him the portrait at the beginning of the book, but he didn't recognise Bishop either. He took a photo of it anyway.

"I'll add it to the search. Maybe it'll give us something."

I headed upstairs to the kitchen, where Ashley was having late lunch, or whatever you call the first meal after you've woken up having slept the morning after a nightshift.

The scent of food made my stomach growl, and I beelined to the fridge. Lunch had been two hours ago, but I was ravenous. Then again, I'd barely eaten half of what had been on my plate at the club, and then I'd cast all those spells. Luckily, Giselle's fridge always contained food in easily microwaveable portions.

Ashley gave me an amused look when she saw my overflowing plate. "Full moon getting to you too?"

I grinned. "No. I had to cast spells with Rupert so that he could find out what's wrong with my spells."

"Did he?"

I'd filled my mouth and had to chew for a moment before I could answer. "There are two or maybe three potential causes, but no immediate cures. But he'll look into it."

Hopefully he found something, because I couldn't keep setting things on fire.

"And how's your detective case going?"

I gave her a recap of what had happened that day. She nodded. "I'm not a fan of the bitch, but I like the idea that she's held by a bloodsucker even less."

"Don't let Luca hear you call them that," I said with a smile, but she brushed my words aside.

"Luca is cool and he knows it." She rose from the table. "I'm off to pump iron. If you need more muscle in your rescue, let me know."

I promised to do so, but I hoped we wouldn't end up needing her.

Food and coffee revived me. My brain less fuzzy, I retreated to the sofa with Charles Bishop's biography of his father. Griselda showed up too, now that Ashley wasn't there, and curled on my lap. Comfortably settled, I read the interesting parts more closely.

Bernard Bishop had married a saint of a woman, if her son was to be believed, who also happened to be a mage. Whether she was also the source of Bishop's information about supernatural beings, the book didn't tell. They had had two sons, Charles and Robert, and according to Charles, both had inherited their mother's ability and become mages. Until then, the book hadn't mentioned magic at all.

At the time the father had published his book, the boys had been in Eton and received their share of the ridicule the father got from his book. Since they couldn't talk about magic in public, the sons had been forced to watch in impotent fury how their father had been ostracised from society.

Charles seemed to be furious on his father's behalf. He was even annoyed with Robert, who wasn't equally incensed. When he'd been old enough to enter society, Charles had picked up his father's quarrel. He'd even tried to challenge Armand de Morganville to a duel over his father's honour, but Armand had died before he had a chance.

That had truly enraged Charles.

Third Spell's the Charm

It was fascinating to read descriptions of his hatred of a man who from his point of view was dead but whom I knew to be alive. It was rather sad too, knowing that Bernard had been correct about Armand being a vampire. But surely Charles, who had to hide being a mage, would've understood that Armand couldn't simply confess to being a vampire.

The book ended with a description of Bernard Bishop's death and the sadness the family had felt for not having his name cleared. The son vowed to do that no matter what it took, and I instantly wanted to return to Rupert's to see if there was a biography of Charles Bishop there too.

I turned to the last page and found two portraits, one of Charles and the other of Robert. My world turned upside down.

I stared at them, blinking, trying to bend my mind to understand what I was seeing. Then I surged up, annoying Griselda, who hissed at me as she dropped on the floor. I made to head downstairs to Luca when his running steps came up the stairs. A moment later, he burst into the kitchen, holding his laptop.

"You never believe who shows up in all the club footage!"

"Maxim Shepard?"

He paused. "How the hell did you know that?"

I showed him the book. There, under the portrait that said Charles Bishop, the unmistakeable face of Maxim Shepard stared at us.

And the other portrait, of Robert, was Adam Finch.

Nineteen

It took forever for Hunt and Dufort to arrive. I had time to change into clothes more suitable for rescuing Danielle—i.e. black running leggings and a long-sleeved tee, with a windbreaker that was red, but it couldn't be helped, and my running shoes.

I wouldn't easily be caught by pursuers if it came to that.

Giselle had time to set the table for afternoon tea. She would've preferred to offer a proper meal for the guests, but she was outvoted.

Amber would've preferred we meet elsewhere, but since she wasn't willing to meet Hunt on his turf and mages' headquarters was out of the question, she settled for being a gracious host.

Formidable, but gracious.

The vampire and the warlock arrived at the same time, having been chauffeured by Ronnie, who walked in behind them looking uncomfortable.

"I'm the muscle," he informed us by way of greeting. I nodded.

"Ashley promised to be muscle too."

He rolled his eyes with a good-natured grin.

Introductions were made, hostile glares were exchanged between Amber and Dufort—the latter was more arrogant than hostile—and then everyone settled at the table to enjoy Giselle's excellent tea.

"This had better be good," Hunt said after taking an approving sip. "I had to leave an important meeting."

"Is the identity of the killer important enough?" I asked, and he cocked a brow.

"Let's hear it, then."

I showed them Charles Bishop's book. "Do you recall the outrage at the end of the eighteenth century that Bernard Bishop faced after publishing *The Fantastical Creatures*?" I asked Hunt. "And especially his attempt to oust you as a vampire and the rest of aristocratic society coming to your defence?"

He blinked. "Can't say that I do."

I stared at him, amazed. "How is that even possible? It caused a huge ado. Bishop was completely shunned in society after that. William Grenville, who later became PM, came to your defence."

Brief emotion flickered over his face, gone before I could identify it. "We went to Oxford together and were good friends until I ... Armand sadly died."

Did that mean Armand had grown up in England? Or had merely pretended to be the correct age?

"Then why did you want the book so badly?"

He shrugged. "It has a copy of a portrait of mine that I've lost."

Huh. I guess that was as good a reason as any.

"This is very fascinating, but surely it's ancient history?" Dufort said impatiently. He had barely touched his tea.

Third Spell's the Charm

"Not for vampires," I said dryly, and Hunt pulled back.

"Are you saying Bernard Bishop is a vampire?"

"No. His sons are."

Dufort's brow cleared, understanding. "Ah, avenging their father's honour?"

"That's precisely it. Charles Bishop, the older son and the author of this book, even wanted to challenge you to a duel, but you'd died before that."

Hunt looked puzzled. "And he's waited over two centuries for it? Surely he could've acted before."

I made a face. "That's the part I don't really understand myself. It becomes even more bizarre if you consider the current identity of the younger brother, Robert."

"And that would be?"

I showed them the portraits and Hunt recognised Adam Finch immediately.

"It appears I was wrong after all..." He sounded more stunned than angry, but at his age he'd probably been wrong often enough to be able to handle it.

"Not necessarily," Luca said. "He wasn't invested in his brother's quarrel with you. If he hated you, he would've done something when you worked together a century ago."

Hunt tilted his head. "Could be. So it's the other fellow who's after me, then? Who is he?"

"The older son, Charles, who challenged you to a duel."

I wished I had drumrolls for a dramatic effect, but I had to settle with a pause while I looked at everyone around the table.

"Also known as Maxim Shepard."

Stunned faces met me.

"Are you sure?" Hunt asked. Luca nodded. "The CCTV footage shows he was in all the clubs."

Ronnie took a closer look at Charles too, and nodded. "I've seen him there."

"So Finch acted to stop Shepard?" Hunt asked and I shrugged, remembering Adam's fury when he heard Sam was dead.

"Or it's revenge for killing Sam."

"Are you saying that he burned his own brother to death?" Amber asked appalled.

That hadn't even crossed my mind. I shuddered. "I hope not."

The others didn't look as convinced.

Kane furrowed his brows, puzzled. "The question remains, why act only now? Even if Charles Bishop lost track of you, surely Finch would've told his brother about you long ago."

I spread my arms. "I have no idea. Perhaps Finch kept it to himself, knowing his brother's hatred of Hunt."

"Then why did he kidnap Danielle?" Dufort asked.

"I have no answers. I only have the players and a plausible explanation for why this is happening."

"Fine. We'll have to ask them ourselves," Hunt stated. "Where do we look for them, then?"

"At Finch's house," Kane said. "We did another trace, and it points there again."

"How did you get past the ward?" Dufort asked, and Kane sneered.

"Natural magic isn't entirely useless."

Dufort sneered back. "It can't be entirely accurate either. There's nowhere to hide in that wreck. We looked everywhere."

Third Spell's the Charm

Kane nodded. "And now we'll look again."

THERE WERE NINE OF us gathering at the end of Finch's street that evening. Hunt and Dufort had personal reasons to attend, and Luca wanted to see his investigation through. Ashley, who'd arrived home in time to come with us, and Ronnie were muscle. Kane, Amber and Giselle were the magic defence.

The only useless participant was me. I had no strength, supernatural senses, or reliable magic. A sensible person would've stayed at home with the cat watching the *Great British Bake Off*, but turns out I'm not sensible. I refused to be left behind.

So had Giselle, when Amber suggested it. "I'm more than a cook!"

Amber had placed a hand on her wife's cheek. "Last time, you almost became a human sacrifice. I can't risk that again."

"What are the odds that that would happen again?"

I'd glanced at Dufort; I couldn't help it. He'd noticed and sneered. It hadn't eased my nerves.

Kane studied us calmly. If he was nervous, or anxious to find his ex-wife, it didn't show. He was still in the suit he'd worn to work, as were Hunt and Dufort. It should've looked odd, considering what we were about to do, but I was accustomed to seeing him in it and it calmed my nerves.

"We're looking for a secret entrance to a hideout. The house itself isn't the likely place, so that leaves the cellar and garage."

"The floor of the house isn't stable," Ashley stated. "They'd be foolish to hide in the cellar."

Hunt tilted his head. "That would make it ideal for the entrance. No one will go there."

"Whether it's there or not, we can't go through the front door," Luca said, pointing at Finch's house. There wasn't anyone guarding the entrance anymore. Instead, the door and windows had been covered with plywood.

Kane nodded. "Magic can do many things, but it can't create an entrance where there isn't one."

"Not without a lot of noise anyway," Dufort added dryly.

Since noise was what we were trying to avoid, we headed to the street below, where Finch's garage was. There was no parking on that street and none of the buildings were residential, so we had no witnesses when our group gathered in front of the double doors of the garage.

Kane's familiar spell revealed complicated wards on the doors. He pursed his lips, studying them. "The protection wasn't this elaborate on the garden side. Surely they wouldn't have bothered with this if the place was truly empty."

Together, the mages removed the wards. Hunt handled the lock, as vampire magic was more suited for those kinds of spells. He pulled the door open, and we held our breaths. But the garage was still empty.

My shoulders slumped minutely, as if I'd hoped that Danielle would be there waiting for us. I made to step in, but Dufort threw an arm in front of me.

"There's something off with this place."

"You didn't say anything last time."

His jaw tightened. "I was too worried for my Danielle to register it properly."

No one questioned him, even though no one else seemed to sense anything. I definitely didn't, but that wasn't a surprise. He reached his hand slowly into the empty space past the doorjamb. Nothing happened.

"Are you sure you're not just suffering from a case of nerves?" Hunt drawled.

Dufort ignored him. He pulled his arm back and studied the emptiness with narrowed eyes.

"An invisible wall?" Kane suggested, but Dufort shook his head.

"My hand wouldn't have gone through."

"Some sort of reality distortion spell?" Amber asked.

Dufort pursed his lips. "Maybe. But it takes a huge amount of energy to maintain, and I don't think Danielle is quite that strong."

Kane shot him a sharp look. "Could there be other mages helping her?"

"This isn't a spell a mere mage could do…"

My gut clenched when the implication of his words sank in. "Are you saying … that Danielle is now a warlock?"

It required a human sacrifice to take the last step.

"She wasn't when she left home."

"It would explain the body found in the fire though," said Luca, voicing what the rest of us were too cowardly to say aloud. Kane's face tightened and Dufort didn't look entirely happy either.

Dufort stepped back, hands propped on his hips as he studied the emptiness. "If this is what I think it is, I'll need blood to bring it down."

We all turned to Hunt, who straightened, dismayed. "I don't walk around with bottles of O+."

"I'll give it," I found myself saying, and the sea of faces turned to me, most of them disapproving. I went on the defensive. "It's the least I can do. I don't have magic or strength, but I can help bring this wall down."

"How much do you need?" Kane asked Dufort, who shrugged.

"Not much. The little mage's blood worked the previous time, so she'll do."

"What previous time?" Kane demanded.

"The time I saved your life," Dufort said with a sneer.

Considering Kane had been unconscious at the time my blood was needed, it wasn't a wonder he had no recollection. He turned to me, and I shrugged.

"Better mine than his." I faced Dufort before I lost my nerve. "How do you want to do this?"

"With as little blood loss as possible."

Good to know.

"Does anyone have a knife?" I asked.

Hunt gave me a slow, suggestive look, his lip curling. "A vampire doesn't need knives to open a vein…"

Shivers ran down my spine and they weren't solely for fear.

"A mage doesn't need one either." Kane held his hand out to me, palm up, and I rested my wrist on it.

He pushed up the sleeve of my windbreaker and made a quick gesture over the vein on my wrist. A tiny wound appeared there, with barely any pain, and blood began to well. I stared, fascinated, as it began to run down to my palm.

"That'll do," Dufort said. "But keep it coming."

We settled into a half circle behind him, with me next to him, offering my cupped palm. Blood was starting to fill it. I could practically sense the mages' disapproval and

Third Spell's the Charm

Hunt's keen attention on Dufort as he dipped a finger into my blood and drew a sigil in the air with it. It was nothing like what the mages used. They shuddered, and I had trouble watching it too, as if the sigil itself were evil.

To my amazement, the sigil remained in place, like it had been drawn on a proper surface. Dufort nodded, pleased with himself.

"*Exactamente...*"

With fast, economic movements that revealed decades of practice, he drew several different sigils in the air, some of them complicated, needing a lot of my blood. When the last one was done, hovering in the air, he nodded at me.

"You can cover that now."

Kane gestured with his hands and the blood stopped flowing. I'd seen him cast this spell before, but it was more impressive when I was the recipient.

Giselle pulled out a first-aid kit from her backpack, cleaned my hand swiftly, and put a plaster on the wound. "Just in case," she said with a grim smile.

Meanwhile, Dufort had begun to unravel the spell that only he could detect. It wasn't flashy or loud. He barely moved his arms, and if there was an incantation he didn't say it aloud. But I could sense energy building, harsh on my skin, like wet hands in freezing wind.

Ashley and Ronnie growled, the sound almost subvocal, vibrating against my body. Others fidgeted, as if trying to escape the uncomfortable sensation.

The sigils of blood began to glow and then they burst into flames, startling us. The abrasive sensation disappeared as the spell took. Dufort clapped his hands together and the interior of the garage became visible.

It wasn't empty anymore. It was full of furniture. From floor to ceiling, side by side with barely room for a slim person between them. Every piece of antique that I'd admired in Finch's home was there, carefully piled on top of each other, with layers of protective cloth in between.

"I did not see that coming," Ronnie muttered. Ashley shook her head.

"Explains why there were no traces of burned furniture in the house."

I'd secretly rued their loss and here they were.

"I knew he couldn't leave all that behind," Hunt said, looking smug for having anticipated this. "But why is it here and not moved to safety?"

"Neighbours would've commented if they'd seen him move all his furniture right before his house burned down," Amber said dryly, but Luca shook his head.

"He's a vampire. All he needed to do was give them new memories."

Kane nodded, his eyes thoughtful. "So why *is* the furniture here, then…?"

"It's to make it more difficult to find Danielle," Hunt stated, studying the furniture. "If your spell tells that she's here, then she's somewhere among this furniture."

Kane stepped into the garage and this time Dufort didn't stop him. Nothing bad happened.

There was a narrow gap between the end tables, dining room chairs, bookshelves, and a beautiful grandfather clock I hadn't noticed when I visited the house. He began to squeeze through it. Dufort's brow furrowed.

"Look for anything you can fit a person in."

Third Spell's the Charm

My money was on the grandfather clock, but Kane had reached the middle of the floor, disappearing from our sight. "Here!"

One by one, we pushed through the gap towards him. There was a tiny open space between the furniture around a seaman's chest with a polished lacquer finish that had likely belonged to an admiral. It wasn't large enough to be comfortable even for a woman as dainty as Danielle, but she would fit in.

"Are you sure that's the right one?" Amber asked. Kane nodded.

"It's the only piece here that has nothing piled on it."

"You'd best check it for wards first."

"Of course there are wards," Dufort huffed. "But are they anything that you can break?"

Kane didn't bother to answer him, and simply unravelled the wards. Had it been me, I would've shot a lofty look at Dufort. Kane merely opened the heavy lid and stared into the chest, his jaw flexing.

"Empty. I guess I was wrong."

"Finch wouldn't have bothered to ward it if it weren't important," Giselle said. She leaned down to look. "A magic wall?"

Kane gestured with his fingers and shook his head. "Nothing."

I pushed closer to look too. "A false bottom?"

"Danielle wouldn't fit under it. The chest isn't large enough," Dufort noted, but Kane reached in and pressed the bottom. It clicked, and opened, as if on springs. There were hinges on one long side and he pulled it all the way up.

Hunt's eyes flashed in that eerie way of his. "Now we're in business."

There was a manhole under it, open and with iron rungs attached to the ancient-looking brick wall. There wasn't enough light to see how far down they stretched, but one thing was certain:

That was where we needed to go.

Twenty

IN SURPRISINGLY SHORT ORDER, considering the size of our group and the tendency of most of them to insist they go in first, we were climbing down the ladder, with a magical light illuminating our way.

Ronnie went first, claiming that if the ladder held him, it would hold the rest of us.

It wasn't a long climb and there was only a small space at the bottom, like an overflow well but without any drainpipes leading in or out. The space barely fit us all, even standing shoulder to shoulder, and Ashley and Ronnie had to bend their necks not to hit their heads.

It wasn't a dead end though. A heavy iron door led out, protected with a basic ward. Kane as the closest soon had it unravelled. Ronnie insisted on going first again.

"I don't think there's anything dangerous there," Amber said, as Ronnie pulled the door open, forcing us to almost stand on each others' toes to give the door enough room. "Otherwise all the wards would've been on the other side of the doors."

Dufort swivelled to her, forcing the rest of us to adjust our places again. "You mean Danielle isn't there?"

Amber shrugged. "If these are her wards, then most likely yes. How else could they have been done if not when she left?"

I tensed when I remembered something. "She isn't the only mage."

Everyone turned to me, which was quite a feat. "What do you mean?" Kane asked.

"Finch is a mage too. Or at least he was before becoming a vampire."

Hunt's power flared, almost suffocating in the small space. "And you didn't think to tell me? Even after I told you those are extremely rare?"

I grimaced, embarrassed. "I completely forgot in my excitement for finally having a solid lead."

"This changes everything," Amber said. "We have to watch our backs too."

"I'll keep the rear," Ashley stated, and Amber nodded.

"I'll be with you, in case a mage is needed."

Ronnie was finally allowed to go through the door. A spiral staircase led down, made of cast iron and surprisingly ornamental, considering it was hidden underground. It looked to be Victorian, so it had been here since the house was built.

There was a tunnel at the bottom, narrow and dusty, with footprints running down it, indicating it had been used recently. There was only one way to go, and Ronnie was halfway down it already by the time I reached the bottom of the steps, his head brushing the ceiling despite bending his neck.

After about a hundred metres, during with the tunnel had continuously sloped down, it began to rise steeply and then ended at a few steps up and a door that wasn't warded for a change. Giselle checked.

Third Spell's the Charm

"I'd begun to think that Finch is paranoid," Hunt muttered as we filed through the door.

There was another tunnel on the other side, perpendicular to the one we'd just exited. Made of brick, it was wide enough for two people side by side, and high enough for Ronnie to stand straight. It looked old, but it was mercifully devoid of cobwebs and rats. All sorts of electric and light fibre cables ran along the ceiling in thick bundles. It led to two directions, and we paused to determine where to go. There wasn't enough dust on the brick floor to give any hints.

"Maybe we should split up," Luca suggested. "There's certainly enough of us."

Kane shook his head. "I'd be happier if we stayed together."

The tunnel began to vibrate, faintly at first and then so loudly we couldn't hear each other for a few moments as what sounded like a train went right behind us, as if through the tunnel we'd just been in. Even knowing it wasn't possible, my legs went feeble.

"Is there a Tube line parallel to this behind the wall?" Ashley asked, when the noise had quieted. "It sounded like it passed above the tunnel we just used."

I perked. "The Waterloo and City!"

"Of course," Hunt said, smiling. "I remember now. This way."

He turned to the right, heading in the opposite direction from where the train had gone, and we followed.

"Why this way?" I had to ask, and he glanced at me over his shoulder.

"Because Waterloo Station is in the other direction."

"Maybe they're there, using the Tube lines," Luca suggested, and he nodded.

"They definitely use them. But that place is too crowded and busy for a proper hideout. Besides, if I recall correctly…"

He marched on, forcing the rest of us to hurry to keep up. Another train passed, towards the City now, making it impossible to speak.

We'd walked almost five minutes when the tunnel abruptly ended, with only a narrow pipe for the cables to continue. A door stood on both sides of the tunnel, one of them towards the Tube rails. Hunt chose the other.

He gestured at the sturdy but old iron door. "Do your magic."

Kane eyed the door dubiously. "Where are we?"

"Underneath the Southbank embankment, near Blackfriars Bridge. Well, the sewers are under the embankment, but this is right next to them. The Tube line continues under the Thames, but this tunnel ends here."

"There are sewers on the other side of the door?" I asked, appalled.

"No, there's a room on the other side."

"That's an odd place for a room," Giselle noted. "Why is it there?"

Hunt smiled, the first genuinely delighted expression I'd seen on his face. "Vaughn, or Adam Finch if you prefer, designed it for a hideout for vampires. He put it in the plans when he drew the Tube tunnel and the builders built it, no questions asked about its purpose. There was a time when every vampire in London knew about this place."

"So if you'd remembered this earlier, we could've rescued Danielle already yesterday?" Dufort demanded, but Hunt only shrugged.

Third Spell's the Charm

"I'm old. I can't be expected to remember everything."

Dufort didn't look happy. He made an impatient gesture with his hand that made power woosh to him and my ears pop like in an airplane. Dust shook from the tunnel ceiling as he removed all protections from the door at once.

"That's one way of doing it..." Kane muttered. Dufort sneered and swept his hand towards the door.

"*Après vous, mesdames et messieurs.*"

"We shouldn't just barge in," Ronnie said when the rest of us were about to do just that. "We don't know what waits on the other side."

"Can you hear anything?" I asked.

He shook his head. "But that can mean many things. Maybe the room is empty, maybe the door is too thick."

Kane nodded. "Everyone, have offensive spells ready—and shields," he added, glancing at me. "Ronnie, you pull the door open for us, just a little, so that we can take a look."

Everyone took their places, spells ready. I began to gather the energy and locate the spark for my shield spell, but before I had it properly up, Ronnie opened the door.

A single dim bulb lit the space on the other side. I barely caught a glimpse between the people blocking the doorway, but what I saw made my heart jump.

Danielle was lying in the middle of the floor, unconscious. There was a small patch of blood by her face, already dried, come from her nose.

Dufort made an anguished sound and rushed in. The rest of us followed, the heavy iron door shutting behind us with a loud bang.

Dufort gathered Danielle carefully in his arms, her prone form seeming even smaller next to his powerful body, stood up, and conjured a portal. Without a glance at us, he stepped through, taking Danielle with him.

The portal closed a heartbeat later. They were gone.

"I DID NOT SEE that coming."

I stared at where the portal had been, my mouth all but hanging open. It had happened so fast I hadn't even noticed where he had taken her, to his home or hers.

Kane stared at the empty space with a disgusted sneer. "I had no doubt whatsoever he would do that the moment he found her."

"If he hadn't hurried away, we could've taken care of her injuries with Amber," Giselle said, turning to her wife, only to startle.

"Where's Amber?"

We all twirled around, but she wasn't in the room with us.

"Ashley's missing too," Ronnie said, his face tightening.

I forced the uneasy flutter in my stomach to settle. "Maybe they were too slow to enter, and the wards came back up when the door closed."

They had kept the rear, but I hadn't paid attention how far behind us. They had entered the wider tunnel, hadn't they?

"Surely they would be banging on the door asking us to open it," Giselle said, but Kane shook his head, looking grim.

"Not if the wards came back up. And there's no saying what kinds of wards they were, the way Dufort demolished them before I had a chance to look."

Giselle paled. "You mean Amber can't break them?"

Ronnie marched to the door. "Then we'll open it for them."

Kane tensed, but before he managed to shout a warning, Ronnie had already planted his hands on the door.

There was a loud bang and a bright flash that almost blinded me. Ronnie was thrown back, the force of the spell launching him halfway across the small room, where he landed heavily on his back, unconscious.

"Now we know what happened to Danielle," Hunt said dryly.

Giselle and I kneeled by Ronnie. I checked the pulse from his wrist, and it was strong. Giselle glided a hand behind his head.

"There's no blood. Hopefully it wasn't a lethal blow to his head."

"He's a werewolf," Hunt said, not very concerned for his employee. "He has a thick skull and great ability to heal."

Ronnie's eyelids fluttered, indicating Hunt might be right. He opened his eyes, but they took a moment to focus properly. Giselle placed a hand on his cheek. "Rest a little. You've hit your head."

His brows furrowed and he began to growl. "I need to find Ashley."

"We'll find her together."

He looked pale in the poor light, and didn't try to sit up. "What happened?"

Kane answered from the door where he was studying the wards. "This is a forceful spell. It's amazing you gained consciousness at all."

"Are they the same than at the cemetery?" I asked, going to him. He'd made the wards visible, and they looked vaguely familiar to me; a nasty creation Blackhart had used to imprison Rupert.

"Yes."

"It took Dufort to break them last time." They'd knocked Kane unconscious, the reason I'd needed Dufort's help in the first place.

His jaw flexed. "And three mages."

And there were only two here. And no Dufort.

"Are you saying we can't get through that door?" Luca asked. Giselle lifted a hand to her chest.

"We're trapped in here?"

"Maybe the wards are easier on the other side and Amber can open it for us," I suggested.

"Unless she and Ashley are unconscious too," Luca said unhelpfully.

I shot him a quelling look, then turned to Giselle. "Call her."

Giselle took out her phone, but shook her head. "There's no reception."

Everyone took out their phones, with the same result. My stomach was beginning to roil with unease. Was it my imagination or were we running out of air? I'd been trapped in an underground vault recently and it had left me with issues.

"Surely there's another way out? A vampire wouldn't have created a hideout that would trap him."

Hunt sneered. "Of course there's another way out. There's a door here."

My knees wobbled with relief as I turned to look. The room wasn't large, and most of it was in shadows, so I hadn't paid attention to my surroundings. The door Hunt

Third Spell's the Charm

was pointing at was the colour of concrete and almost disappeared in the wall.

"Maybe it's heavily warded too," Luca said, voicing my concern.

Kane crossed the floor to it, gathering magic. "Only one way to find out."

Turned out, it wasn't warded at all, or boobytrapped with spells. He reached for the handle, but Ronnie halted him.

"I'd best go in first."

He wasn't entirely steady on his feet when he pushed up, but the determined look on his proud face was such that we didn't dare to object. He pressed an ear against the door and listened carefully before opening it.

The room on the other side was longer than the first but not much wider. It couldn't be, wedged between the tube tunnel and the sewers. It smelled damp, like an old cellar, and it was cold there.

My nose clogged instantly, but not so Ronnie's. His nostrils flared and he walked determinately into the room, only to pause, baffled.

"I can smell a vampire here."

The room was empty, as far as I was able to detect, but I'd been around magic long enough to know that my eyes could be deceiving me.

"It has to be Max Shepard, hidden with magic."

Kane and Giselle walked into the middle of the room, and both made identical gestures with their hands.

"Here! In this corner." I pointed at where I'd seen the air shimmer next to me.

The mages came to me and repeated the gesture. In a blink of the eye, the empty corner was empty no more. A hunched, unconscious figure of a man became visible, and it was definitely a vampire.

But it wasn't the vampire I'd been expecting.

"That's Adam Finch!" Luca exclaimed.

What the hell?

"What is he doing here?" Kane asked, amazed.

"Can you revive him?" Hunt said, crouching by the unconscious figure.

Together, Ronnie and Luca manoeuvred Finch to lying on his back on the floor. Giselle made a quick examination and shook her head.

"There's nothing visibly wrong with him. It must be a spell."

Kane pursed his lips and gestured with his fingers. "Nothing I can immediately detect."

"Is it warlock magic?" Luca asked. Kane gave him a questioning look.

"Why do you say that?"

Luca spread his arms. "It must be Danielle who did this, right?"

"So Finch takes her captive," Hunt said, "but she manages to incapacitate him and flee, only to be knocked out by the super ward on the tunnel door?"

"That is the likeliest explanation." Kane kneeled by Finch and tried to detect the magic again, only to shake his head. "I don't know this spell at all. Either it's warlock in origin, Danielle's own invention, or it's very old."

"Danielle was never one to study old spells," Giselle noted, abandoning her attempt to revive Finch by slapping his cheeks.

"But where is Shepard, then?" Hunt asked.

Luca shook his head, his lips in a grim curl. "At the morgue."

Third Spell's the Charm

"No, he can't be," Hunt stated. "The body belonged to a human, not a vampire."

A nagging sensation that I'd forgotten something important made my entire body tense. I must've made a noise because Luca gave me a questioning look.

"What's wrong?"

I spoke slowly, formulating the idea as I went. "If both Danielle and Finch were unconscious here … then who warded the route down?"

Everyone tensed, then slowly turned to look around the empty room.

"There's that other route out," Kane said. "Finch left Danielle here, went out the way we came in, then came back here the other route."

"But the question is, why would he go through such trouble?" Hunt stated. "I think there's an unknown warlock at play here."

I finally remembered what I should've from the start. Blood fled my face, making me sway a little. "Finch isn't the only vampire mage. Maxim Shepard is too." My only excuse for forgetting it was that I'd thought him to be captive.

I sensed magic build behind my back and turned around just in time to see Shepard step out of thin air, dressed like he'd been when I'd seen him last, unconscious in Danielle's car. The red leather jacket with the billowing shirt and tight jeans didn't look theatrical, they looked threatening.

"So good of you to remember my existence. I would like to make a small correction though. I'm not a mage. I'm a warlock. And now you die."

He curled his fingers into a fist and a ball of black energy formed into it. I had no time to react before he attacked.

Twenty-one

THERE WAS A LOUD BOOM WHEN the ball hit the floor where Hunt had stood only moments earlier. The impact made me dizzy, and for a moment I struggled to understand what I was supposed to do.

Then a solid presence stepped between me and Shepard.

"Shields, Phoebe," Kane shouted, already flinging an energy ball at Shepard. It hit the vampire warlock's shield without causing damage.

The others had recovered from Shepard's surprise appearance and were attacking too, but everything they threw at him stopped at his shields. The spells ignited at least a metre from him, so his shields had to be extremely thick. Luca tried to flank him, only to run into the shield at the side too, unable to get past. He only barely managed to dodge the spell Shepard flicked at him.

Shepard was on full offensive, and every spell he flung was aimed at Hunt, forcing him to lunge and jump, the vampire's shields non-existent. He had vampire speed though, and the spells missed every time.

I was the only inept person here, with no combat skills, magical or otherwise. A flush of fury rushed through me for my uselessness as I watched my friends fight for their lives. I gathered energy for a spell, concentrated as best I could, and flung a wind spell at Shepard.

The inevitable fire my spell caused didn't even reach his shields before dying. I was in serious risk of igniting my friends though. Berating myself for not learning to cast spells when I had the chance, I gave up trying to help.

It was five against one even without me. But the room was too small for this kind of magic battle. The old walls were reverberating with the force of energy balls, making dust and mortar rain on us. It was only a matter of time before one of us would be hit, if not by magic then by falling bricks.

"We have to retreat to the smaller room!"

"What's the point if he can portal there?" Luca asked, his attention on Shepard.

"You go, Phoebe," Kane said, a little breathless for all the spells he had thrown at Shepard. He had already used a lot of energy for breaking the wards on our way here. "And take Giselle with you."

Her focus tightly on Shepard, throwing balls of energy at him, Giselle didn't look like she was ready to retreat. But her attacks came far in between, and the spells were getting smaller.

"Giselle! Help me move Finch."

She heard my plea and abandoned her attack. Crouching to avoid Shepard's onslaught, she hurried to me.

"You go out first, I'll shield our retreat," she said, barely managing to get the words out, her energy almost spent.

Third Spell's the Charm

I grabbed Finch under his arms, but his prone form made it difficult to get a good hold. I couldn't dawdle though to get a better grip. I began to drag him towards the open door to the smaller room, Giselle helping by lifting his legs.

"Oh no you don't!"

Shepard flicked an energy ball at us. It hit Giselle's shield, causing her to drop to her knees and lose her hold on Finch. My grip slipped too, and Finch's upper body dropped on the floor. His head thumped heavily on my foot.

Ouch.

I ignored the pain. Behind Giselle, Shepard was aiming another spell at us. I took a hold of the upper sleeve of Giselle's jacket and yanked her aside just as the spell hit the spot where she'd been. She fell, a bewildered look in her eyes, and I almost collapsed on her.

I pushed back up, pulling her with me. "Leave him," I ordered Giselle, who'd been about to take Finch's legs again, and pulled her after me towards the smaller room. "He won't harm his own brother."

I hoped.

The room was filling with dust and smoke from the spells, but Shepard was already aiming another fireball at us, not tiring at all or slowed down by the spells thrown at him.

The spell never hit us. Behind him, a low dark form had slinked past his shield. Ronnie! As a wolf. Silently, without alerting Shepard to his presence, he sank his fangs into Shepard's calf muscle.

With a scream of pain, Shepard's concentration broke. His shields disappeared, and the men attacked. But their aim was vastly off, barely reaching him, and it only forced

Ronnie to let go of Shepard's leg and retreat or be hit.

Kane prepared another spell, but it barely formed, his energy all but spent. Shepard didn't wait for it to hit but created a hasty portal and lunged through. Kane's spell sailed through the empty spot where Shepard had been and hit the wall.

It was over, but we hadn't won.

EXHAUSTED, KANE DROPPED to his knees and leaned on his hands before lowering down until his elbows rested on the floor. His sides were heaving hard. Magic was always draining, but a magic battle squeezed every last drop of energy from a mage.

Luca sat down, leaning on the wall, elbows resting on his bent knees, his head dropped. Even Hunt was sweaty, his expensive suit worse for wear for rolling on the dusty floor, but he didn't look quite as exhausted as the other two. Ronnie sat on his haunches, still in wolf form. His shirt was clinging to him, as he hadn't taken time to strip before shifting, but his jeans had come off.

Giselle and I leaned against the doorframe for support. I wasn't as exhausted as the rest, having only tried that one spell, but adrenaline leaving my body made my knees weak.

"Is everyone all right?" I asked, pushing up. Giselle made to follow suit, but I gestured for her to sit. "Rest now. We need to move soon."

I crossed the floor to the men. Luca was the closest and I put a hand on his shoulder. "How are you feeling?"

He gave me a tired smile. "I could use a pint of blood, but I'll be fine in a moment."

Hunt leered at me. "I could use some too, if you're donating."

Third Spell's the Charm

I'd donated enough blood tonight, so I rolled my eyes and went to Kane, who had managed to sit up. His smile was assuring, but his eyes were tired.

"I'm fine. Just a little winded." This from a man who thought nothing of running ten miles before work every morning.

I didn't point out that the last time he'd done a magic battle he'd slept for hours afterwards. I simply offered him a hand and helped him up. He dusted the knees of his trousers, tugged his once crisp shirt back to its place, and removed the tie he had still been wearing, putting it into the pocket of his trousers. Then he looked around.

"We need to leave before Shepard returns."

Hunt nodded. "How often can a warlock create those portals?"

"I have no idea, but he probably needs to take care of the wound in his leg first, so I think we have a little time."

Ronnie looked smug, insofar as a wolf could.

"What should we do with Finch?" Giselle asked leaning over the unconscious the vampire.

"We have to leave him," Hunt ordered. "We're none of us in any shape to carry him."

"We can't leave him," I protested. "He's the only one who knows where Shepard might have gone to."

Hunt glared at me. "I doubt we've seen the last of him. He'll find us."

"Can Ronnie shift back?" Kane asked.

"Probably..." I eyed the wolf, who shook his head. "But two shifts in a short time will drain all his energy and he won't be able carry anyone either."

Ashley usually slept a day after a shift.

"We have to find Ashley and Amber," Luca said. "Is there any way to get back to the tunnels?"

Hunt nodded. "It's this way."

He went to the opposite end of the room to where we'd entered. In the corner was a manhole with the hatch open.

"Finch probably came in through here," I noted aloud.

"Or Shepard fled through there, if it was him who knocked Finch out instead of Danielle," Kane pointed out.

"Except he can create portals."

"Are we assuming that Finch isn't a warlock too, capable of portals?" Luca asked. "If a human sacrifice is what's needed for it, a vampire shouldn't find it too great a threshold to cross."

We turned to look at the prone form at the other end. "Should we bind him with magic just in case?" I asked.

Kane's jaw flexed. "I would if I had anything left, but I fear I won't make it out of here if I cast one more spell."

Ronnie yipped. He went to Finch and settled on the floor next to him. I nodded.

"Ronnie will stay. He won't be able to make it down the ladder in his wolf form anyway."

Hunt didn't waste time arguing but climbed down the rungs. One by one the rest of us followed, more or less shakily. There was only a small tunnel at the bottom, so low that we had to crouch to be able to go forward, and our shoulders brushed both walls.

It wasn't a long tunnel, maybe fifteen metres, but the backs of my thighs were burning by the time we reached the end. I eyed the rungs up with misgiving, but there was no escaping it.

Hunt went up first, pushing open the manhole at the top of the ladder, but he didn't climb out. "It opens

Third Spell's the Charm

straight to the side of the Tube tracks. We'll wait for the train to pass and then everyone has to climb out as fast as possible."

Marvellous.

We didn't have long to wait. The train passed right above us, making the tunnel shake. The noise was awful, and the vibrating in my chest made it difficult to breathe.

The sound hadn't even passed when Hunt climbed out. "Hurry. The trains on this line are few and far between, but there's no reason to dawdle."

Giselle went next, and then it was my turn. My thighs were protesting every rung up, but I gritted my teeth and managed to pull myself out of the manhole decently fast. A moment later Kane emerged too, with Luca keeping the rear. It was warmer in this tunnel than in the others and it smelled of iron and ozone and that familiar Tube smell that wafted out of the tunnels when you waited on a platform.

Hunt closed the hatch. "Hurry. We need to cross the tracks. Do not touch the one closest to us and the third one. They're live."

There were four tracks in front of us, with barely enough room between the wall and the closest one to avoid touching it, but at least they were fixed on the tunnel floor and not a metre up in the air like outside the platforms. Gingerly, I stepped over them.

We reached the other side without anyone becoming electrocuted. There was even less room between the wall and the closest track, but at least that one wasn't live. Hunt hurried down the narrow path until he reached a door.

"This one's better not be warded..." he muttered. He reached for the handle and pushed the door open.

The rails began to hum.

"Hurry."

Heart in my throat, I ran through the door with the others, and Hunt closed it behind us. A moment later, the train went past.

"That was close," Luca said. I was leaning against the tunnel wall, trying to force my heart back to its customary place, and could only nod.

We were back in the original tunnel. Amber and Ashley weren't there. Part of me was concerned, but mostly I was relieved they weren't lying unconscious on the floor, knocked out by the wards on the door.

"They must have gone back to the garage when they couldn't get through the door," Giselle said.

We hurried down the tunnel back the way we'd come. All the doors were still open and nothing or no one hindered us. My leg muscles loosened enough that I was able to climb up the staircase and the ladders up to the garage.

It was empty—save the furniture. There was no sign of Ashley or Amber. Disappointment brought acid to my mouth.

"What now?"

Everyone looked around, as if the women would miraculously appear.

"We can't go after Shepard without reinforcements," Hunt said, taking out his phone and starting to write a message. Giselle took out her phone too.

"I'll call Amber. Maybe she's somewhere with reception."

She pressed the call icon and waited for the call to go through. A moment later, Amber's ringtone chimed somewhere near.

Third Spell's the Charm

Luca cocked his head. "They're in the garden!"

"Why would they be there?" Giselle huffed, but her brow cleared in relief.

"Moreover, how did they get there?" I asked, eyeing the furniture blocking the way to the door towards the garden.

We pushed past the furniture, climbing over and under until we reached the back door. With a relief, we exited into the garden. It was already dark, but one thing was immediately clear:

There was no one there.

"What the hell?"

You didn't often hear Giselle curse, but I understood her frustration.

Hunt leaned down to pick up something. "Is this Amber's phone?"

My heart stopped and I could practically sense others tense too. "Where are they?"

"There are only two places, the house or the cellar," Kane said, heading across the garden, with no sign of exhaustion in his long strides.

I wasn't eager to enter either of the places, but if the women were here, they might be in trouble. Why else would Amber's phone be left behind?

Hunt reached the cellar before Kane, but he only peeked in, took a sniff, and retreated. "Empty."

I hadn't waited for his verdict. I was already at the back door, which hadn't been covered with plywood. It was dark inside the house now that the front windows and door were boarded over. Kane was right behind me, and he sent in a mage light, smaller than usual, his energy all but gone. But it was enough to see by.

My gut froze.

In the middle of the floor, sitting back-to-back, immobilised by magic, were Amber and Ashley. They were conscious and angry, but unable to speak. With a gasp, Giselle rushed past me towards them, only to become immobilised too.

Kane forced his light to become brighter. Behind the women, pale with pain and a snarl on his face, was Maxim Shepard.

"Let's finish this."

SHEPARD WAS OUTNUMBERED again, but we were exhausted. Kane could barely maintain the light spell, let alone create energy balls. The vampires weren't faring much better, and our muscle was incapacitated. I hadn't miraculously turned into a ninja mage.

"Why don't we handle this just the two of us," Hunt said behind me, entering the house. "I'm the one you want."

"What, pistols at dawn?" Shepard asked with scorn.

Hunt shook his head. "We're both from the era when duels were fought with swords."

"I don't see any swords here."

"That can be arranged. Just let the women go and we'll settle this like gentlemen."

Shepard sneered. "You've never been a gentleman."

"I was a nobleman," Hunt said with a careless shrug, taking a step forward.

"Don't move!"

Shepard's command was meant for all of us. Kane and Luca had begun to round him from both sides, and I'd moved away from the line of fire between him and Hunt. But he hadn't tried to immobilise us. That had to mean he'd reached his limit of people he could hold.

Third Spell's the Charm

I began to gather magic for my shields. They had blocked some spells Rupert had flung at me, and though I doubted they would hold against Shepard's attacks, they were better than nothing.

A burst of magical energy behind me broke my concentration. Hunching my shoulders, fearing an attack, I turned to look just as Finch stepped out of a portal, awake but bleary. He was supported by Ronnie in his human form again, tired but stalwart against Finch's weight.

Just as the portal began to close, Hunt lunged through. I caught a brief glimpse of Dufort's aggravated face on the other side before the portal disappeared.

Hunt had left, and it wasn't to fetch the swords.

"You have to stop this insanity, brother," Finch said, his voice weak but determined. "It's been over two hundred years."

"You never understood!" Maxim cried. "Armand de Morganville made a fool of Father and he never had to pay. And then he turned out to be a vampire, just like Father said—and you knew!"

Adam took a step closer to his brother. Maxim lifted his palm up, the spell gathering on it, still large and powerful, halting Adam.

"I only found out a century later. I hoped you'd forgotten your folly by then."

"I'll never forget!"

Evidently. But I managed to keep that to myself.

"And what do you think you're achieving with all these attacks? You've killed innocent people."

Maxim sneered. "I'm a vampire. All my victims are innocent."

"At your age, you wouldn't have to kill to feed."

"I'm a warlock. A few deaths don't really bother me."

Adam paled, as if he hadn't known that. "They don't really bother Hunt either. But they bother me."

"You've always been weak."

Maxim threw the spell he had been gathering, and I leaped to a side to avoid being hit. But he wasn't aiming at his brother—or me. He hit the floor in front of Adam, making the damaged floor sway. One more hit like that and we would all plunge into the cellar.

Adam, for his part, had lunged forward and was now face to face with Maxim, only the immobilised women between them. If the brothers started to fling spells, there was nothing Amber and Ashley could do to avoid being hit.

But Shepard's attack had made him lose control over the binding spell holding Giselle. She sank slowly on her knees, her legs refusing to move her to safety.

A powerful spell was forming on Adam's palm that he held behind his back. It covered his hand and continued up his forearm, the colour turning more intense until it reached pure white of extreme heat. If he hit anything with that, we'd all be hurt—or worse. And this time Danielle's wards wouldn't keep the fire from spreading to neighbouring houses.

As fast as I could, I began to build my shields again. They wouldn't help much, but they'd be something.

"There's nothing weak about loving someone," Adam said calmly.

"Are you talking about Sam? Because I took extra pleasure in killing him." Maxim's face lit up with such glee that I wanted to punch him. "You should've seen the look on his face when he realised what I was about to do."

Third Spell's the Charm

Adam's face was calm. Too calm, but his brother didn't notice it. Behind Adam's back, the hand on which the spell was still growing stronger squeezed into a fist.

"Let's end this, for both of us, permanently."

"What?"

"You took the one person who made this long, miserable life worth living from me. I have no reason to live anymore, and you certainly don't deserve to."

Adam pulled his glowing arm from behind his back and reached for his brother's chest, unheeding of the spell Maxim had built and was aiming at him.

"No!"

I hadn't consciously decided to shout, but it halted the men, if briefly. I didn't care about Maxim, but I didn't want to witness them annihilate each other, or hurt my friends in the process.

"Sam is alive, Adam. Hunt made him a vampire."

Adam swivelled around, just as another portal opened behind me. Hunt stepped out with Sam, as if he'd waited for the perfect moment to make an entrance.

Sam looked healthy and strong in jeans and a T-shirt, a far cry from the half-dead person we'd secreted out from the morgue.

"Adam!" he cried.

Adam didn't have time to react to Sam's sudden presence when Maxim already threw the spell he had been gathering at Sam—or Hunt, I couldn't tell.

Unthinking, I stepped in front of Sam, my shield tight in front of me. Maxim's spell hit it, igniting a wall of fire inches from my face.

But I was prepared for it and my shield held. Maxim kept pouring energy into his attack, ignoring the spells Kane and Giselle were flinging at him, and the fire kept burning, eating away my shield fast. I reached inside me, digging deep for the source of my magic, pulling every drop of energy I had and forcing it into the shield.

"You will not harm him again!" I ground out between clenched teeth. Something moved inside me, like pieces of a puzzle or tectonic plates settling to their rightful places. The shield formed anew with an almost physical click, and the fire disappeared.

The attack spell didn't stop, and my shield held, with Sam crouching against my back for cover.

Adam had recovered from Sam's sudden appearance. He turned to Maxim and placed the hand holding the spell on his brother's chest, calmly, almost caressing, as if saying goodbye. In a flash, Maxim was gone. Not even a pile of ash remained.

The spell attack I had been leaning against vanished so abruptly that I dropped on my knees, panting with exhaustion, Sam barely manging not to trample me. The shield disappeared.

Adam stared at the spot where his brother had been. Then he shook himself and faced us. His smile was hesitant where he looked at Sam.

"Are you truly ... here?"

Sam uttered a distressed sound and rushed across the sodden, swaying floor to Adam, who spread his arms and pulled him into a tight hug.

A warm hand landed on my shoulder. "Are you all right?" Kane asked, face full of concern. I nodded, tired but triumphant.

"My shield held!"

He smiled, warm and proud. "I saw. Welcome to the world of spellcasting, Phoebe."

Epilogue

EVERYTHING WAS WRAPPED UP amazingly fast. Maxim Shepard was gone and if it saddened Adam to have killed his brother, he didn't show it. His attention was on Sam, who couldn't stop talking and telling him everything that had happened to him since waking up at the morgue.

"At first it was the worst thing in the world to be a vampire, but then Morgan told me you're one too. I can't believe you didn't tell me."

"I'm sorry, but I couldn't."

Amber and Ashley had been freed when Shepard died, the magic binding them disappearing with Shepard. Giselle finally found her legs and rushed to Amber and the two hugged as tightly as Sam and Adam.

Amber told us Shepard had caught them in the garden when they were trying to find another way into the tunnels. Ashley was aggravated that she hadn't been there for the battle.

Ronnie wrapped an arm around her shoulders. "Don't worry, sis. I handled everything."

"Where did Dufort come from?" I asked him and he shot me a grin.

"Hunt told him to fetch us. He showed up, revived Adam, and whisked us here, then went to fetch Sam with Hunt."

Dufort wasn't around anymore, and I could only hope he and Danielle were gone for now. He had been helpful, but having a warlock around was unnerving and there would likely be a price to pay.

Hunt looked pleased with himself. "I guess you're officially off the hook," he said to Luca, whose eyes grew large.

"You didn't seriously still think all this was my fault?"

Hunt only shrugged and headed across the garden. The rest of us followed at a slower pace. I'd never used this much magical energy before and I could barely stand up. Kane wrapped an arm around me, and I leaned against him for support, unheeding that he was exhausted too.

I slept the entire Friday, and likely would've slept through Saturday too, but we had the auction, so I dragged myself out of bed and into proper clothing. I was at the shop well before the courier from the security service brought the maps.

Kane arrived early too, as elegant and put together as always. But there were lines of exhaustion around his eyes, and instead of warding all the display cases like he had planned, he only placed small wards at the doorways, which would activate if someone tried to steal the maps. Even that seemed to tire him.

But we had the security the insurance company had demanded. And just to be on the safe side, Luca acted as security too, elegant in a black-on-black suit. We would've asked Ronnie or Ashley, but it was the full moon and they'd gone somewhere safe to prepare for it.

Third Spell's the Charm

The auction was the success we had hoped it would be. To my amazement, Hunt showed up and bid for a map. He didn't win, but it didn't seem to upset him.

Afterwards, he invited us to a dinner at his place. We always celebrated a successful auction in a nice restaurant and since we had no reason to refuse, we accepted—except Mrs Walsh, who had a prior engagement.

Hunt's home was as it had been the first time. Either I was over my fear of him, or I was too tired to be intimidated by him anymore, but I was perfectly calm as I entered the marble foyer and walked down the short hallway.

A surprise waited for us there.

"Miss Peaches!"

It was indeed her, in a form-hugging pink evening dress, wig of real auburn hair falling to her waist, and her makeup perfect. She looked fabulous.

I skipped down the steps to her, and she pulled me into a tight hug. Then it was Luca's turn. Only when I was released did I notice Adam there too, looking proud and happy as he watched her.

"I'm so happy you could come," Miss Peaches gushed after we'd settled down at a long dining table at the other end of the room and a caterer had brought in the dinner. "We're leaving London for a while, and I wanted to thank you for everything you've done for me."

I looked at her bemused. "We didn't do anything."

"But you did. You tried to find my killer and you were good enough to try to locate my next of kin. We only met that night. You didn't have to do that."

A faint blush rose to my cheeks. "Well, we did leave you for dead in the nightclub…"

She made a sympathetic moue. "That must have been so awful. Luckily I don't remember much of it. Only Maxim appearing in my booth and coming on to me. I can't even remember if I pushed him away or if I let him. I wasn't that drunk, but apparently he mesmerised me." She paused and sighed. "I can't wait to learn to do that."

"As long as you won't try your skills on me."

She let out a pealing laugh.

The evening was long and surprisingly joyous. It was impossible not to be cheerful around Miss Peaches. She seemed to be over the worst shock about her new life, and I was happy for her. I would miss her while she was gone. In vampire terms, "a while" probably meant a couple of decades.

I therefore didn't hesitate when at the end of the evening she begged us to go to clubbing with her. She told Adam hated those places, and she didn't want to force him. "I need to face the place where I died or I'll be forever traumatised."

Luca was eager to go too, and while Kane wasn't as enthusiastic, he filed into the taxi with the rest of us. Hunt came too, to give us access to the VIP area of his club and to keep an eye on Miss Peaches on her first outing among the general public as a newly fledged vampire.

Soon we were seated on the mezzanine above the dance floor of the gay club with frilly, colourful cocktails Miss Peaches insisted we order. The VIP area was empty save for us, and even Kane relaxed, leaning against the backrest of the low sofa, his legs stretched before him. I noticed his feet tap to the beat under the table, but I knew better than to try to drag him onto the dance floor with us.

Third Spell's the Charm

The dancing exhausted me faster than it should have. I left Luca dance with Miss Peaches and returned to our table, where Kane was sitting alone, nurturing a whisky. He patted a spot next to him, and since I was a little tipsy and too tired to care about a proper boss-employee behaviour, I complied, sitting so close I could feel the heat of his body through our clothing.

I was suddenly wide awake.

He leaned down to be heard over the music, speaking close to my ear. "How are you feeling?"

I cleared my throat that had gone dry when his breath brushed my earlobe. "Fine. I'm … fine." And since I didn't want it to be an idle boast, I picked an empty glass from the table. "Look!"

Magic came easily to me now. I had no idea what had happened during the confrontation with Maxim Shepard, but it was as if a dam had broken inside me. I focused and the spark answered. With a practised twist of my fingers, I conjured water inside the glass.

Nothing caught fire!

I gave a triumphant look at Kane, showing him the glass half full of water. But his attention wasn't on it. It was on my face, his eyes meeting mine, searching. A faint blush rose to my cheeks and my pulse sped up.

"That's wonderful," he said warmly. "I'm proud of you."

He leaned closer, his eyes holding mine as his lips met my mouth. And then he kissed me.

Acknowledgements

I wrote this book during the Covid pandemic, which—while unpleasant—left me and mine relatively unscathed. Still, life disrupted takes its time to find a way to a new normal. I escaped to reading and writing. This book is the result. I hope it brings you joy. Thank you for reading.

I'm always grateful for my husband for his support, but during a time when both were working from home all day, every day, I came to appreciate his patience. I learned some too.

As ever, I want to thank my sisters for being a sounding board to my ideas. Turns out, messaging is an effective alternative, when you can't meet face to face.

As I'm writing these acknowledgements, we're a week into a war in Europe that we wished never would come. I hope there's a peace by the time the book comes out. I want to thank the online writing community for simply being there, sharing their experience in these odd times. I hope we're all heading towards better ones.

About the Author

SUSANNA SHORE is an independent author. She writes *Two-Natured London* paranormal romance series about vampires and wolf-shifters that roam London, *P.I. Tracy Hayes* series of a Brooklyn waitress turned private investigator, and *House of Magic* paranormal mysteries set in London. She also writes stand-alone thrillers and contemporary romances. When she's not writing, she's reading or—should her husband manage to drag her outdoors—taking long walks.

If you want to find out when Susanna's next book comes out, subscribe to her newsletter on her website

www.susannashore.com

Made in United States
North Haven, CT
03 April 2023